The Best of

enterprise incidents

THE MAGAZINE FOR STAR TREK FANS

Edited By James Van Hise

PIONEER BOOKS, INC.   LAS VEGAS, NEVADA

THE BEST OF ENTERPRISE INCIDENTS

Ten years after *Star Trek* first aired, ENTERPRISE INCIDENTS was born. It was in 1976 and while it was hardly the first *Star Trek* fanzine, it has long been regarded as one of the best.

There was an average of only 2,000 copies printed of those early issues but the magazine quickly developed a following of faithful fans who could tell that we really loved what we were doing.

I published the first eight issues myself, whereupon it was picked up by another publisher, although I stayed on as editor. The material in this book is drawn from issues as early as #2 and spans the life of *Star Trek* itself as well as of the magazine.

The magazine exists now only in the form of the book you're holding, but since several pieces in this book appear here for the first time, one could hardly say that ENTERPRISE INCIDENTS is defunct. Rather it has just reorganized into a new format so that we can continue exploring the broad scope of the world of *Star Trek*.

—James Van Hise

Founding Editor, ENTERPRISE INCIDENTS

April 1990

The relationship between the cast and their fans is a major factor behind the incredible endurance and resurgence of STAR TREK after its cancellation.

Here we see "Sulu" and "Scotty" together with their fans.

Why are you reading this book? Why is STAR TREK still so popular after all these years? Let's discuss the reasons why.

The Endurance of Star Trek

by James Van Hise

"Like Spain's Francisco Franco, *Star Trek* has been fatally dead for a long time. Now and then the mortuary shoots an electric current through the corpse, and the resultant spasm releases yet another manual or quiz or convention or novel or book of fan fiction or what-have-you, but after nearly a decade there's little life left in the old cadaver."

—Gil Lamont
& James K. Burk
DeLAP'S F & SF
REVIEW
(March/April 1978)

This statement reflects the feeling a lot of science fiction fans had in 1978 regarding the increasing presence of *Star Trek*. They looked down on the television series, choosing to dismiss the preponderance of interest in it and ignoring the fact that *Star Trek* attained an existence beyond the phosphor dot TV image or the larger than life images of the silver screen.

It touched a common chord in many individuals who, ironically, spent years quietly enamored with the series, unaware they shared a bond with countless strangers. Then they happened upon a fan magazine or walked into their first media convention, and unexpectedly found themselves at a reunion of a family they'd never known existed.

Before *Star Trek*'s return to the screen in 1979's *Star Trek: The Motion Picture* and its soaring sequel, *The Wrath of Khan*, a groundswell of anti-*Star Trek* backlash brewed. Most of it arose from the attitude that "those people" were "invading" the otherwise sedate and pristine atmosphere of science fiction conventions. On the restroom wall at one San Diego Comic Con, someone with an artistic bent crafted a large drawing of a woman copulating with a decaying Vulcan corpse. Scrawled

7

above it was the rallying cry "*Star Trek* is dead."

As I write these words so many years later, I wonder how often those erstwhile critics have seen the new versions of *Star Trek* which have emerged since 1978.

What these people reacted to was the continuing popularity of a TV show which seemingly died in 1969. No longer new or current, it was supposed to stay respectfully dead. How many of these detractors read and collected novels by long-dead authors? They pursued interests' others could deem defunct, yet to them, *Star Trek* was just a TV show in perpetual rerun.

Something recycled can still be appreciated. Long after their deaths, people still widely read the works of H.P. Lovecraft, Robert E. Howard, E.E. "Doc" Smith, Edgar Allan Poe, Clark Ashton Smith, Edgar Rice Burroughs, H. G. Wells and Jules Verne. Sir Arthur Conan Doyle died in 1930, but Sherlock Holmes wins more readers today than ever before. Every year someone takes pen in hand to create an "untold" tale of London's most famous sleuth. Nicholas Meyer, the director of *Star Trek II*, wrote two best-selling novels chronicling strange tales of Baker Street's resident detective, *The Seven Percent Solution* and *The West End Horror*. Harlan Ellison is fond of pointing out that, "Any book you have not read is a new book."

I raised some of these points in a letter written in reply to the remarks quoted at the beginning of this chapter. If I hoped for a reply, I was sadly disappointed. I did not know I bore witness to the silent death throes of that venerable magazine. Now it's gone, not unlike a mist which quietly dissipates at the first light of a morning sun, while the supposed corpse of *Star Trek* remains amazingly healthy.

Why is it healthy? Why did it endure after the last set was struck? A special *something* at its core created a whole greater than the sum of its parts; a magic that struck a responsive chord. The series offered something people searched for but couldn't find again until *Star Wars* emerged in 1977. The successes of the two are inextricably linked.

Optimism played the keynote in both *Star Trek* and *Star Wars*, as we faced the future with eyes looking to the stars, no matter the squalor that lay at our feet.

When *Star Trek* premiered in 1966, the Space Race surged ahead at full steam. Yet the dream of reaching beyond the mortal confines of our world began to seem just that — a hopeless dream. As America plunged deeper and deeper into Southeast Asia, the future no longer burned as brightly. When friends and relatives returned home in body bags, the dream itself seemed to die.

Then came *Star Trek*, promising a future that worked. The first view of the starship Enterprise astonished us as we beheld a sight from out of time!

Slowly we met the Enterprise crew. Captain Kirk, noble and almost fearless, yet tortured by every death of a crewman under his command. Leonard "Bones" McCoy, the ship's doctor and captain's close friend who often played devil's advocate. These two interacted in a very human way.

Despite obvious exhaustion, "Bones" addresses his fans at a convention in Louisville in 1976.

At the perimeter, cool and austere, was always Spock. Spock the alien. Spock the enigma. Singled out for special treatment both because he was second in command and because of his alien heritage. An outcast in charge, making cool decisions about emotionally charged issues.

At the core of the stories stood a sense of being; a living presence. People thought and bled, made mistakes and held personal philosophies. In "The Naked Time," their most deeply rooted doubts and feelings emerged screaming to the surface. No other science fiction series using a continuing cast had tried this before. Even more astonishing, none have tried it since.

When *Space: 1999* premiered in 1975, we hoped for something of equal substance. It didn't have to be *Star Trek*; it just had to be good. When instead it proved dreadful, there was a violent backlash. *Space: 1999* (or *Space: 1949* as one critic aptly named it), was so awful we felt betrayed. There was no excuse for something to be *that* bad; no reason for the awful writing and the wooden direction. Much the same hope and subsequent resentment was unleashed by *Battlestar: Galactica*. Networks found that you couldn't promise an oasis and then reveal a desert.

Star Trek characters pursued lives of their own. Each new script added another layer of characterization. You could believe they continued to live after the end credits, waiting for us to tune in again. We grew to understand them and recognize their human qualities.

Captain Kirk and the others stood as idealizations. We knew that when push came to shove they would do the right

thing. While fans talk about the fine characterizations of Kirk, Spock and McCoy, they don't really possess the normal human foibles of you and me. At worst they might show anger or make a snide remark, but they'd always meekly apologize afterwards. When it came to ethical choices, they were infallible.

A case in point is Harlan Ellison's "The

City On The Edge Of Forever." In the scene where Edith Keeler dies, Harlan wanted to have Kirk try to save her, despite knowing his action could destroy his future. Kirk would have failed, but would have *tried* to save her. This is Harlan's version of the story, which won the Writer's Guild Award. Series creator and executive producer Gene Roddenberry felt Kirk wouldn't act like that. Kirk would always do the right thing, no matter how painful. Roddenberry rewrote Ellison's screenplay and Captain Kirk deliberately prevented McCoy from saving Edith's life. He experienced great anguish, but did the right thing. While Ellison's screenplay solved this problem by having Kirk bring Edith back to the future, Roddenberry had a point to illustrate. Although the characters of *Star Trek* endure, and act more believably than those of *Lost in Space, Space: 1999* and others, they are still idealizations. The characters appear genuine because it's the only attempt to have continuing characters in a science fiction series act like human beings. They agonize over decisions, struggling with philosophical and ethical principles. By contrast, on *Battlestar: Galactica*, human characterization includes a little boy becoming almost catatonic over the death of his pet, yet accepting with equanimity the death of his mother.

In the days following the cancellation of *Star Trek* in 1969, a revival wasn't even dreamed of. Fans were grateful for any mention of the show, however tepid. One example is the brief dismissal given it by John Baxter in his 1970 book *Science Fiction in the Cinema.* He devotes only three paragraphs to *Star Trek* and, although two of the three are fairly generous in their praise, he fails to understand the series. While praising "The Menagerie," he criticizes the use of stock footage and formula situations. He singles out "Patterns of Force" (Nazi Germany) and "A Piece of the Action" (Chicago in the Thirties) while ignoring more representative episodes such as "City On The Edge Of Forever," "This Side Of Paradise" and "Mirror, Mirror." He completely fails to understand what *Star Trek* was trying to accomplish. While he singles out "Charlie X" for praise, he never mentions the obvious inspiration of Robert Heinlein's *Stranger in a Strange Land.* Heinlein wrote the story about a human child raised on Mars who learned fantastic powers (such as making things "go away") from non-corporeal beings. One of the last things Charlie says in the episode when he's pleading to stay is that the creatures that raised him don't even possess real bodies he can touch.

Baxter's biggest oversight is that he makes no mention whatsoever of the characters. Episodes like "Where No Man Has Gone Before" and "This Side of Paradise" initially hooked me on the series. Yet it didn't take long to realize something new was being done with continuing characters. The characters weren't interchangeable, but cared about each other. This, above all else, accounts for the endurance of the series. Fifteen years before *Hill Street Blues* and half a decade before *M*A*S*H*, this show offered an ensemble of characters who attained levels equal to the finest moments of these more recent shows. William Shatner was the supposed star, but he needed the other actors to play off. Mr. Spock began life as a secondary character and fascinated the viewing audience until they demanded more of him. He quickly reached a level of importance equal with Kirk, and this duo has symbolized *Star Trek* ever since. This human element was the heart of the series, and Baxter missed it entirely.

Paramount distributed publicity shots of their heroes, the crew of the starship Enterprise, to eager fans.

Brian Aldiss, a fine British science fiction writer, also missed it. In his *Dream Makers I* (1980, edited by Charles Platt), he said ". . . the negative side is that the media have a great grip in the States, and so you get hogwash like *Star Trek*, with its bright—well, it's not very bright, actually—this tinsel view of the future, and the galaxy, which has to be optimistic. I did once manage to see an episode all the way through, and at the end Captain Kirk says to the— the chap with the ears— 'Well, this proves that the galaxy's too small for white men and green men to fight one another,' and Spock nods and says, 'That's right,' and they clap each other on the shoulder, and up comes the music. Well, what Spock should have said was, 'Why the f—k shouldn't white men and green men fight together? Of course there's plenty of room.' Liberal platitudes do distress me. And yet I remember having this argument with some quite high-powered chaps, and they said, 'That's a very subversive point of view, you may think these are platitudes, but they actually do a lot of good.' But I still think that science fiction should be subversive, it shouldn't be in the game of consolations, it should shake people up, I suppose because that's what it did to me when I started reading it, and that was valuable. It should question things. I have to say, I owe a lot to John W. Campbell and his damned editorials in *Analog*. I believe that you should challenge everything, you know? Occasionally, in my more manic moods, I still carry that early Campbell banner: Science Fiction should tell you things you don't want to know."

It's unfortunate Aldiss based his opinion of *Star Trek* only on an episode like "Arena" or "Let That Be Your Last Battlefield," but he does raise an interesting point, Star Trek was never subversive or dangerous in the views it purveyed. The closest Star Trek ever came to being subversive was in the third season when "The Enterprise Incident" was conceived as a take-off on the Pueblo Incident. It was originally supposed to have concluded with Kirk questioning whether spying is ever morally justified.

Even as we enter the 90s, Star Trek: The Next Generation stays on the same safe path blazed by its 60s ancestor.

Star Trek was ultimately a safe port; a place of optimism which said, "There will be a future," while ignoring the thorny and deeply troubling social issues which still plague us. By doing so, it served a purpose, one which continues to this day.

The Menagerie" remains one of the ten most popular episodes of Trek Classic. The contribution of actor Jeffrey Hunter is one of many reasons this story remains captivating.

Star Trek's First Captain: Jeffrey Hunter

by James Van Hise

Before William Shatner became Captain James T. Kirk in the pilot episode "Where No Man Has Gone Before," there had been another captain.

Star Trek's first pilot is usually referred to as "The Cage," although it contained no actual episode title on film. The pilot starred Jeffrey Hunter in the role of Christopher Pike, captain of the U.S.S. Enterprise. NBC rejected "The Cage" as "too cerebral." However, rather than turning down the series outright, the network requested another pilot. Unfortunately Jeffrey Hunter was no longer available.

Jeffrey Hunter was born Henry H. McKinnies, Jr. in New Orleans on November 25, 1927. He changed his name upon commencing his film career, a common practice before the current era of realism struck Hollywood and actors began to retain un-star-like names.

A talent scout for 20th Century Fox discovered Jeffrey Hunter in 1950. At the time, Hunter was performing in a UCLA campus production of *All My Sons*. He immediately signed a long-term contract.

Hunter made four films released in 1951, although only in the fourth one, T*he Frogmen,* was he cast in a starring role.

In most of his films, Jeff played the clean-cut, all-American boy, although in 1955's W*hite Feather* he portrayed an Indian, hardly his most unusual role.

In 1961 he played Jesus Christ in the all-star Hollywood production of K*ing of Kings*. Hunter cared about reviews and although publications such as V*ariety, The New York Times a*nd F*ilms in Review* delivered kind notices, T*ime's* review was scathing. They referred to the film as "I Was A Teenage Jesus."

Hunter's always youthful appearance both helped and hindered him. While it insured leading man roles for many years, it also limited him to those roles. Approaching forty, he often said, "This face of mine. Shouldn't the ravages of time be doing something to it?"

Although his hair began to turn prematurely gray, he always kept his youthful good looks.

Unlike film stars who disdain television, Hunter enjoyed it. It gave him a chance to play different parts than the ones constantly offered in movies.

In 1964, Jeff's own production company put together the series *Temple Houston,* based on the life of Sam Houston's lawyer son. It aired in the 1964-65 television season, but was seen earlier as an NBC replacement series. Unfortunately, this show didn't last long either. (*TV Guide r*an an article on Hunter in its January 11, 1964 edition—noted for collectors in the "audience").

Other TV work done by Hunter included a guest starring appearance on the debut episode of *The F.B.I.* in 1965, as well as one on 1966's *The Green Hornet* , in the episode "Highway To Death."

At this time—1964 actually— he acted in the first *Star Trek* pilot for Gene Roddenberry.

Hunter brought ease and determination to the role of Christopher Pike, adding to the intensity and realism of the story. He captured the grimly determined commander who rarely smiled and carried the burden of command heavily. Yet it was a character of depth and believability, as well as power. Had he remained as the captain in the series, I think it would have been a bit different as Hunter came across as a brooding man of intense emotional reactions. Where Captain Kirk was a man of action, Captain Pike was a man of violence. When he gains the upper hand over the Talosian Keeper, he threatens the Keeper's life. His threatens in menacing tones, such as "Stop this illusion or I'll twist your head off!" "Would you like me to try that theory out on your head?," and "To start by burying

you?" Captain Kirk would not have been in character saying those things. If Hunter had remained with the cast, the scripts would have reflected his powerful, domineering Captain Pike.

Alas Hunter did not remain as he once more became involved in doing feature films.

Lest you suspect Hunter allowed earlier roles to influence his choice of later ones, the man who played the Biblical Christ in 1961 performed a nude scene (from behind only) in his last released film, 1969's *Sexy Susan Sins Again.* The film received less than enthusiastic reviews.

In May of 1969, Jeffrey Hunter returned from filming in Spain, where he had been knocked down in an accidental explosion and injured his head. As a result, he suffered from dizzy spells and it was apparently one of them which caused his death. He was found unconscious at the foot of a stairway in his home. Apparently he stumbled at the top of the stairs and fell all the way down. Rushed to Valley Hospital, he underwent brain surgery and died. He was only 41 years old. Had he remained with *Star Trek* for the three years it ran, he never would have been in Spain making a film in early 1969. Such is fate.

While Jeffrey Hunter never achieved superstar status, his much admired talent is sorely missed.

THE FILMS OF JEFFREY HUNTER

1951: Fourteen Hours, Call Me Mister, Take Care of My Little Girl, The Frogmen

1952: Red Skies of Montana, Belles on Their Toes, Dreamboat, Lure of the Wilderness

1953: Sailor of the King

1954: Three Young Texans, Princess of the Nile

1955: Seven Angry Men, White Feather, Seven Cities of Gold

1956: The Searchers, The Great Locomotive Chase, The Proud Ones, A Kiss Before Dying, Four Girls in a Town

1957: The True Story of Jesse James, The Way to the Gold, No Down Payment, Gun for a Coward

1958: Count Five and Die, The Last Hurrah, In Love and War, Mardi Gras

1950: Sergeant Rutledge, Hell to Eternity, Key Witness

1961: King of Kings, Man Trap

1962: No Man is an Island, The Longest Day

1964: Gold for the Caesars, The Man From Galveston

1965: Brainstorm, Murieta, Dimension 5

1967: A Witch Without a Broom, A Guide for the Married Man, The Christmas Kid

1968: Custer of the West, The Private Navy of Sergeant O'Farrell

1969: Sexy Susan Rides Again

Let's take a closer look at an unusual story of personal sacrifice and liberation set against the backdrop of a future where anything is indeed possible. . . if you put your mind to it!

" The Menagerie "

an analysis by James Van Hise

The first year of *Star Trek* offered many fine episodes. One stands out above even such favorites as "City On The Edge Of Forever" and "This Side Of Paradise": the series' only two part episode, "The Menagerie." Originally designed to use existing footage to cut costs and save production time, the episode became an inspiration on many levels.

"The Menagerie" explored the background —or backstory, as Hollywood calls it— of the series. It offers the viewer insight into the early years of the starship Enterprise. We see a rather peculiar Spock, one perhaps even more devoted to his captain, Pike, than the Spock we are familiar with is to James Kirk. Spock's scheme to save Pike from the awful life of a hopeless cripple, even at the peril of Spock's own life, bears witness to this devotion. This act also shows a deep compassion the Vulcan would never admit to.

Spock doesn't even bring Kirk into his confidence. The plan plays to its fullest as Spock uses a fictional court martial to carefully reveal his reasons to Kirk, as well as to Star Fleet Command. Admittedly the story never reveals whether the transmission from Talos IV was Spock's idea or that of the Talosians who don't wish to see harm come to

Spock for his selfless deed.

The integration of footage from the first *Star Trek* pilot with sequences involving the new cast is flawless with one exception. Shortly after the landing party beams down to Talos IV, there is the now-memorable scene when Spock smiles! This is totally out of character as Roddenberry evolved Spock in the second pilot "Where No Man Has Gone Before." It is curious for its presence. That this is now a popular scene does nothing to alleviate the inconsistency.

A bit of commentary Gene Roddenberry slipped through while Captain Pike was being punished by the Keeper rarely commands notice. In the sequence, Pike plunges into Hell, which the Keeper describes as being "from a fable you once heard in childhood." It was subtle, and yet effective and meaningful commentary.

A common question is whether Jeffrey Hunter played the crippled Captain Pike as the grotesque (but excellent) make-up reveals a resemblance. That's what they wanted. Even if Jeffrey Hunter was still alive it would have been cost prohibitive to have him play such a minor role. The actor who sat immobile the entire time was Sean Kenney.

15

"The Menagerie" epitomizes *Star Trek*. It offers all the elements that make the series memorable: action, adventure, drama and, finally, optimism. When Pike has been freed in the final scene, if only in his mind, a feeling of triumph and exhilaration is shared with the *viewer*. The viewer is sure they have truly experienced something marvelous in this story; that they have touched the wonder and the beauty which was *Star Trek* at its best.

NOTE: The complete and unedited full color version of "The Cage," from which much of "The Menagerie" was structured, is now available on Paramount Home Video.

Majel Barrett (Roddenberry) portrayed the minor character of Nurse Christine Chapel in STAR TREK. Yet for "The Cage" she was no less than second in command as "Number One." The network forced the change fearing audiences wouldn't accept a woman in so commanding a role.

This episode implied a dark side not only to our heroes, but to the universe of Star Trek!

" Mirror, Mirror "

an analysis by James Van Hise

When the second year of *Star Trek* rolled around, the series had already explored the personalities of the main characters. "The Enemy Within" had examined the possibilities of an "evil" Captain Kirk. As interesting as such an encounter was, it couldn't compare to negative counterparts of the entire Enterprise crew and the Federation itself.

The alternative world theme appears often in science fiction. *The Twilight Zone* explored the possibilities more than once and the feature *Journey to the Far Side of the Sun* took a different approach to the same idea. None of them explored it as deeply as the *Star Trek* episode "Mirror, Mirror."

The author of the episode, J erome Bixby, was not new to the world of science fiction. He had been an SF writer for several years and had even written for the highly respected SF series *The Outer Limits*. In "Mirror, Mirror," Bixby explores a parallel universe Kirk, McCoy, Scotty and Uhura find themselves thrust into. There is an obligatory scene of the alternate universe counterparts on "our" Enterprise, but it shows how ill equipped they are to cope with our world. Mr. Spock is keeping them from doing mischief.

The shock of materializing in an alien yet familiar environment stuns them. Kirk, true to form as commander, quickly recovers.

An interesting point involves the beam-up sequence. Just before beaming up from the planet's surface, Kirk closes his communicator and puts it away. Yet when they partially materialize in "our" Enterprise, he is still holding the communicator as if speaking into it. When they materialize in the alternate universe Enterprise, the communicator is no longer in his hand. It is only on a rare occasion that *Star Trek* made a faux pas involving continuity, but it is interesting to note when they did.

Although Spock intrigues in regular episodes, the malevolent tinge given the personality of the bearded Spock instills pure fascination whenever he is on screen. He is like our Spock and yet he is not. When we see the Spock of our universe again in the closing sequences, it is somehow disappointing, as if an extra spice is missing.

The theme of the "Captain's Woman" is well thought out. In the parallel universe, the Captain is not expected to be almost inhumanly asexual regarding a crewmember. (Remember Kirk's plaintiff confession in "The Naked Time?")

"Mirror, Mirror" did much more than provide the crew with beautiful uniforms and a parallel existence. It also examined the strengths and weaknesses of our own universe's Enterprise and crew.

17

Many talented directors worked on Trek Classic, and this chapter gives them their due, detailing their accomplishments both in and outside this series.

The Star Trek Directors

by Dennis Fischer

Television, it has been said, is a producer's medium. In the dramatic arts, the world remembers writers for their plays, directors for their films, and producers for their television shows. Obviously a producer has a strong effect on what the viewer sees on his screen. *Star Trek* had good producers: in Gene Roddenberry, Gene Coon and Robert Justman. This is not to slight Fred Freiberger, but most fans noticed a decline in quality after he took over with the third season.

Still, what appears on screen is largely the responsibility of the director. He takes a writer's script and, by guiding the camera and the actors' performances, provides the visuals that you see. (Aided, of course, by the actors, set designer, costumer, make-up men, composer, special effects artists, etc.) In television, a director has little time to prepare, does what he has to do, and then leaves. He rarely has a continuing connection with a show, though there are, of course, exceptions.

In addition to having an excellent cast and production staff, *Star Trek* was fortunate to have talented directors. The task of this article is to bring to your attention some of the men responsible for enhancing (or detracting) the many episodes of *Star Trek*.

Robert Butler directed "The Cage," the famous first *Star Trek* pilot and he may have had a hand in the second half of "The Menagerie" which utilized footage from "The Cage." Butler made a mark with an early episode of *The Fugitive* and later became a regular director for *Mister Roberts, Hogan's Heroes* and *Batman*. His direction of "The Cage" was crisp and clean rather than flashy, a style which added an air of reality to this early show. One interesting moment showed the Enterprise from the outside and tracked in towards the bridge via an effective matte shot. It was as if you could see *through* the hull of the Enterprise. It establishes that the ship is traveling through outer space and that this is the story of the people who command her, without using one line of dialogue. Butler also effectively communicates the Talosian ability to read minds and generate illusions. Under his direction, Jeffrey Hunter is not as appealing a commander as Shatner, but he is strong, intelligent and resourceful.

The added time given a pilot episode does show. The detailed alien landscape surpasses that produced for the rushed weekly schedule. For the pilot, Butler tried to direct a superior science fiction film on a low budget with limit-

Allen Koszowski's portrait of Spock, the favorite of many STAR TREK fans. The stoic Vulcan brought an alien air of mystery to the series.

ed time. In all respects he succeeded admirably.

He would later direct the television movies *Death Takes a Holiday*, the third *Blue Knight* pilot (for which he won a well deserved Emmy), *James Dean, Mayday at 40,000 Feet, In the Glitter Palace* and *Lacy and the Mississippi*. After *Star Trek* he directed episodes of *Mission: Impossible, Gunsmoke, Kung Fu, Hawaii Five-O* and *Columbo*. He also directed the unfortunate *Strange New World*, the third attempt at the *Genesis II* pilot after Roddenberry had left the project. This third try had John Saxon as Dylan Hunt and PAX coming to earth after hibernating on an orbital space station (with Enterprise-like bridge noises courtesy of Glen Glenn Sound). They encountered a long-lived race that used clones for replacement parts but overlooked the possibility of senility. The intelligent premise was ruined by execrable execution. They found another culture where park rangers continued to protect an animal preserve long after it had lost meaning for them. This led to a memorably bad line. After kidnapping a female member of the Pax party, a native bargains for a flame-thrower with the offer: "You give me fireshooter, I'll give you woman." Butler also directed four Disney features, some with a science fictional slant (*Guns in the Heather, The Barefoot Executive, The Computer Wore Tennis Shoes* and *Now You See Him, Now You Don't*).

James Goldstone began his career as a film editor and then became a story editor on *Court of Last Resort*. This led to his debut as a director on the show. He directed numerous episodes of *Highway Patrol, Sea Hunt* and *Dr. Kildare*.

In 1963, he became a regular director for Gene Roddenberry's *The Lieutenant* series. For *The Outer Limits* he directed "The Sixth Finger" in which David McCallum grows an extra digit in the process of rapidly evolving himself. For the same series, he directed both parts of "The Inheritors" wherein an

alien kidnaps unwanted handicapped children to take them to a better world. These were two of the best episodes of *The Outer Limits* and demonstrate Goldstone's affinity with science fiction. He also directed "The Brain Killer

The Best of
ENTERPRISE INCIDENTS

19

Affair" for *The Man From U.N.C.L.E.* and several episodes of *Voyage to the Bottom of the Sea.*.

When NBC decided to bankroll a second *Star Trek* pilot (a highly unusual move at the time), Goldstone directed "Where No Man Has Gone Before." It sold the series. He duplicated this trick by directing the selling pilot of *Iron Horse*, which he co-created. *"Where No Man Has Gone Before"* was more action-adventure than its predecessor, but it certainly did not lack in ideas. The aired episode omitted a prologue describing the Enterprise leaving the solar system. This is the only episode for which William Shatner didn't recite his usual opening narration. DeForest Kelley is totally absent, with Paul Fix instead as ship's doctor. Despite these differences, it was from this episode that sprang the *Star Trek* we know and love. The episode quickly defines the characters and immediately plunges into a unique blend of drama, science fiction and characterization.

A pre-2001 *Gary Loc*kwood and a young Sally Kellerman both give good performances as the guest stars. Future director Hal Needham was Lockwood's stunt double. Goldstone admirably presents the two sides of Lockwood's nature, his human half and his possessed state. Spock admits to human emotions for the first time, indicating the beginning of his long friendship with Kirk. Overall, this was one of *Star Trek*'s best efforts.

Goldstone's other *Star Trek* episode, "What Are Little Girls Made Of," is far less effective. In fact, it is thoroughly uninvolving. From the appearance of the cast twisting away on the android table in the blooper reel, they must

have had a good time. They do not communicate it to the audience. There have been worse episodes, but few as forgettable.

Goldstone has continued to direct television, but since the Sixties most of his energies go towards Universal's films. His first film was *Jigsaw*, followed by *A Man Call Gannon* (a remake of the TV movie *Man Without a Star*). Other films include *Winning, Brother John,* the touching *Red Sky at Morning, The Gang That Couldn't Shoot Straight, They Only Kill Their Masters*, the fun but disappointing *Swashbuckler*, the thriller *Rollercoaster* and Irwin Allen's *The Day the World Ended* (nothing like a modest title for old Irwin, eh?). He recently directed the ABC/Walt Disney television miniseries, *Earthstar Voyager*.

Lawrence Dobkin directed only one STAR TREK episode, "Charlie X." It's the best work he's ever done. A minor actor in the Fifties, Dobkin became a regular director on *Dr. Kildare* and *The Rifleman*. His introduction to science fiction probably came from his being one of the main directors for *My Living Doll*, a *My Favorite Martian*-type sitcom about a man and his push-button female android. His sensitive handling of D.C. Fontana's script and good direction of Robert Walker as Charlie made "Charlie X" one of the most touching *Star Trek* episodes. Small wonder that Dobkin was later to become a regular director for *The Waltons*. He also directed "The Pal-Mir Escort" episode of *The Six Million Dollar Man*. Dobkin's direction is generally about average, but with the exception of "Charlie X," never distinguished.

Leo Penn has done a lot of television. Perhaps his best work is his direction of the *Harvest Home* mini-series based on Tom Tryon's novel. He brings out strong performances from actors. Before *Star Trek* he directed for *The Alfred Hitchcock Hour* ("Anyone for Murder"), *Voyage to the Bottom of the Sea* ("The Cyborg"), *Lost in Space* ("There Were Giants In The Earth"), *The Girl From U.N.C.L.E.* ("The Little John Doe Affair") and numerous episodes of *Slattery's People* and *I, Spy*. His direction of Richard Matheson's Jekyll and Hyde tale, "The Enemy Within" is quite good. Shatner's performance borders on the edge of going too far (a typical danger with Shatner) and his brandy-guzzling, eye-rolling evil self could have become laughable, but it's not. And when this evil self is at the opposite extreme, crying for a return, Kirk's inner vulnerability is revealed without being ridiculous. Roddenberry has claimed that he has been asked to show this episode at several psychiatric institutions because of its intelligent portrayal of the dual nature of man and the inherent need for both good and evil.

Penn has since directed enjoyable episodes of *Ghost Story* ("The Summer House"), *Columbo* ("Any Old Port In A Storm"), *The Bionic Woman* ("Jaimie's Mother") and for other television favorites such as *Little House on the Prairie* and *Marcus Welby, M.D.* Apart from *Harvest Home*, he is particularly noteworthy for "Wedding March" (for *Cannon*), "Cry For The Kids" (for *Kojak*), and the *Testimony of Two People* mini-series.

Marc Daniels, along with Joe Pevney, may be considered *the Star Trek* di-

rector. Having met him at a convention, I know he has a love for the show further evidenced by his writing "One Of Our Planets Is Missing" for the animated series. Purists might grumble that the episode is similar to "The Doomsday Machine" which Daniels directed. The first two *Star Trek* movies derive from Daniels' episodes, "The Changeling" and "Space Seed." Before *Star Trek*, Daniels had directed the two part episode "The Like Machine" for *Dr. Kildare* and "The Finny Foot . . . ", "The Shark. . . ", "The Secret Sceptre. . . " and "The Love Affair(s)" for *The Man From U.N.C.L.E.*. Daniels demonstrated that he could mix humor with action and drama, and this was equally true of his *Star Trek* episodes.

His direction of "The Man Trap" looks a little rushed, but is otherwise fine. Uhura's meeting with Vince Howard offers a nice character moment quite unusual for sixties television. Daniels' next assignment, "The Naked Time," is even better. Story editor John D.F. Black filled this episode with moments in which each character reveals something about themselves when pushed to extremes by Psi 2000 contamination. The opening scenes on the chilly Psi 2000 are appropriately eerie and Tormolen's disease escalates everything both comically and disastrously. "Court Martial" was another good if somewhat uncinematic episode (though Shatner telling everyone that the sound will be boosted by one to the eighth power is still embarrassing. Why didn't somebody catch this?) Daniels' direction of the new footage for "The Menagerie" maintains a sense of tension and mystery throughout. Roddenberry skillfully blended the new material with "The

Cage," resulting in one of *Star Trek*'s best episodes, a winner of the Hugo Award. The character of Khan was treated better in Daniels' "Space Seed" than in *The Wrath of Khan* where Ricardo Montalban plays him as a simple madman. In the original he is a dynamic, compelling personality whose philosophy as well as actions oppose Kirk's. This makes him a more interesting antagonist. The idea of a superior being is not always easy to convey, but Daniels and Montalban do it well. McGivers shows scant motivation, weakening the episode.

"Who Mourns For Adonais?" and "The Changeling" are both weaker episodes, suffering from poor scripts. "Mirror, Mirror" remains one of the best directed. Daniels selects his camera angles on the alternate universe Enterprise to allow the ship's interiors to look familiar but slightly altered. They feel different because we view them from a different perspective. He effectively exploits our own familiarity with the sets to create a feeling of unease. "The Doomsday Machine" features a superb performance by William Windom as Commodore Matt Decker. As an episode, it ranks as one of the best. It possesses drama, tension, suspense, action, special effects and the idea of a doomsday machine, first introduced to the public in *Dr. Strangelove*. Both "Mirror, Mirror" and "The Doomsday Machine" were nominated for Hugo Awards.

"I, Mudd," however, is a mess. Initially a delight with the actors ad libbing and hamming it up, on repeated viewings it becomes apparent that the actors are having much more fun than we are and that the story is both trite and dull. This

may possibly by attributed to rewrites right up until the time of production. The same thing might have happened with "A Private Little War" which was plagued by various production problems. For a typically anti-war show, "A Private Little War" surprisingly provides a rationale for U.S. involvement in Vietnam and does so in a simpleminded and hamfisted manner. Incidentally, the episode did produce some wonderful bloopers.

Daniels returned to form with "By Any Other Name" where he and the actors bring life to Fontana's character touches. The idea that the Enterprise is leaving the galaxy never to come back is not as dramatic as it should be, but Daniels wisely concentrates on the touches of humanity that make this episode one of the most enjoyable. He also brings out the humor in "Assignment: Earth," *Star Trek*'s unsold spinoff pilot. Teri Garr has since made it to the big time, but the essence of Garr's comic character can be found in this episode. Robert Lansing dominates the story and makes an intriguing if not too warm hero. It is sometimes pleasant to speculate on the SF series that might have been. Daniels' last effort for *Star Trek* was the atrocious "Spock's Brain," but the fault for that cannot be laid at Daniels' door. "Spock's Brain" was written by Gene Coon as a comedy before Fred Freiberger came on and decided that he wanted *Star Trek* to be pure action-adventure (i.e. no comedy scripts). As "Spock's Brain" had already been ordered (and probably written), an attempt was made to turn it into a serious action/adventure episode. You may judge for yourselves how well this turned out.

After *Star Trek*, Daniels worked on *Mission Impossible* ("Elena"), *Search* ("Live Men Tell Tales"), *The Man From Atlantis* ("The Death Scouts") and *Kung Fu* among others. He also directed Roddenberry's second *Genesis II* pilot, *Planet Earth*, which had a heavy-handed "battle of the sexes" plot that did not go over well with the networks or the audience. (e.g. "All men are dinks.") His work on *Gunsmoke* and *Marcus Welby* is worth noting.

Vincent McEveety is best known for his work on television westerns. He did two stints as a director on *Star Trek*. His first was in 1966 when he did three good episodes: "Miri," "Dagger of the Mind" and especially "Balance of Terror." The second stint was in 1968 when he directed three bad episodes: "Patterns Of Force," "The Omega Glory" and "Spectre of the Gun." His directorial quality does not vary as widely as these episodes would suggest (the reason for the qualitative differences lies more with the scripts than the director.) The unrealistic semi-set for "Spectre of the Gun" (later copied in "The Empath") was quite unusual for the commercial television of that time and still is today, but the show suffered the same fate as "Spock's Brain" when an intended comedy was altered to become "serious." "Balance of Terror" on the opposite end of the spectrum, works well because of the numerous conflicts it presents and its reliance on "submarine warfare" techniques. That episode may have inspired the Reliant-Enterprise battle in *The Wrath of Khan*. "The Omega Glory" could have been a good episode. The first three quarters presents some interesting ideas (the Enterprise crew *could* become infected

with a disease that will prevent them from ever returning, biochemical warfare *could* result in longer lived descendants for those that survive and implies that the cost wouldn't be worth it), however the finale obliterates the episode's good points and the direction echoes the high-handedness of Kirk's patriotic lecture, complete with flag-waving.

Joseph Sargent started out as a minor actor and became a director on *Lassie* where he did numerous episodes. He directed several *Man From U.N.C.L.E.*'s, including "The Alexander The Greater Affair" which was released theatrically as *One Spy Too Many*. His sole *Star Trek* was "The Corbomite Maneuver" in which the Enterprise was impressively dwarfed by the Fesarius. The show was above average, missing mostly with the dubbing of the mannikin and, of course, Clint Howard as Balok. ("Have some Tranya, Captain.")

Sargent's work has been much more interesting since his involvement with *Star Trek*. Such work includes the pilot for *The Immortal*, the pilot of *The Invaders*, the tv movie *The Night That Panicked America*, and the films *Colossus-The Forbin Project, Tribes, The Man, White Lightning, The Taking of Pelham 1-2-3, MacArthur, Golden Girl* and *Jaws-The Revenge*.

Gerd Oswald was a stylist who was hailed by critic Andrew Sarris as being an obscure but delightful director, and unfortunately that is what he remained. Oswald learned how to work fast, use his camera well and seemed to be drawn to material with an anti-fascistic theme. (Guilt over his German background?) His work for *Ford Theatre*,

General Electric Hour, Playhouse 90, Rawhide, The Fugitive and *The Outer Limits* is mostly praiseworthy. His direction of Harlan Ellison's "Soldier" stands out and helps to make that particular episode a memorable science fiction classic. His films (*A Kiss Before Dying, The Brass Legend, Crime of Passion* and *Fury at Sundown*) are all good, though the same can't be said of all of his later projects. In the mid-Eighties he translated and subtitled Peter Lorre's only directorial effort, *Die Verloren* (*The Lost Ones*) for showing at the Filmex film festival in Los Angeles. His last work was directing for the new CBS *Twilight Zone*, including their adaptation of "The Star" by Arthur C. Clarke. Gerd Oswald died in 1989.

Oswald directed two *Star Trek*'s, one of them being the underrated "Conscience of the King." Oswald knew how to direct the camera, set the lighting, block the actors and direct their performances for maximum effect. Though utilizing Shakespeare can be very tricky, Barry Trivers' script does it well. The episode revolves around a mystery (who is doing the killing? Is the actor Karidian really the notorious Kodos?), character revelation and an essential moral problem (would Kodos' solution have been condoned if the grain shipment hadn't come?). *Star Trek* loved to deal with these kinds of moral and ethical questions. Arnold Moss gives a superb performance as Anton Karidian. Barbara Anderson, with a light gleaming from her eye, gives the proceedings the right touch of madness. The script is enriched by its approach of performing a play within a play just as the play being performed,

"Hamlet," features a play within a play to get at the essential truth. Kirk's doubt echoes Hamlet's. While not one of the most exciting *ST* episodes, it is one of the best.

"The Alternative Factor," Oswald's other *ST* episode, is not so satisfying. Again there is a mystery (what is going on with Lazarus?), an anti-fascistic theme (how do you prevent a madman from destroying the universe?) and a noble self-sacrifice which are all in keeping with the spirit of *Star Trek*, but "The Alternative Factor" is another case of "it could have used another good rewrite." Still, the visual depiction of the Lazarus' struggle is interesting and the from-the-rear shot of the Enterprise firing on the planet is both memorable and unique in the angle chosen.

Still, Oswald is more likely to be remembered for his good films and his *Outer Limits* episodes with their effective camerawork and lighting derived from the German expressionist tradition.

Joseph Pevney started in Hollywood as an actor, appearing in such films as *Nocturne, Body and Soul, Street With No Name* and *Thieves' Highway*. He directed action adventure films for Universal, including *Six Bridges to Cross, Foxfire, Away All Boats, Congo Crossing, Tammy and the Bachelor, Man of a Thousand Faces* (the Lon Chaney biopic starring James Cagney), *Twilight of the Gods, Cash McCall, The Crowded Sky, Portrait of a Mobster* and *Night of the Grizzly*.

Apart from *Star Trek*, Pevney's television work has consisted of some fine westerns, "Memo From Purgatory" for the *Alfred Hitchcock Hour* wherein James Caan plays Harlan Ellison in the adaption of his book on juvenile delinquency. For the same series, Pevney also directed "Starring the Defense," "A Nice Touch," "The Trunk," "Bonfire" and "One of the Family". Other television work includes "The Adonis File" for *Search*, "The Glory Shouter" for *The Name of the Game*, the "Meet Dracula" episodes of *The Hardy Boys* and the tv movie *Who is the Black Dahlia?*

However, his fourteen episodes for *Star Trek* remain his most memorable work. His first episode for the show was "Arena" which set up a simple battle between Kirk and a Gorn captain filmed at Africaland USA. The episode was an intelligent adaptation of the classic Frederick Brown story and for once it seemed that the Federation might not have been in the right. In "Return of the Archons," Pevney does manage to quickly evoke the oddness of the Beta III community and the excesses of the "Red Hour," but the episode is not one of the better entries in the series. "A Taste of Armageddon" is an improvement in which an overbearing Kirk once again flagrantly violates the Prime Directive, but its point of recognizing the nastiness of war is well taken.

By "Devil In The Dark," Pevney starts showing real talent and a genuine feel for the show. The unseen "monster" that creeps up on people is well done, and when glimpsed the Horta is no disappointment. Still, the problem disappears vary rapidly after Spock learns some Horta culture (sorry, I couldn't resist). "The City On The Edge Of Forever", rewritten by Gene Rodden-

berry from Harlan Ellison's original script, is generally recognized as the single best episode of the show and with good reason. It captures the drama, the humor, the moral conflicts and the speculative concepts that made *Star Trek* popular. Our heroes are friendly, likable and humorous, but are also capable of great depth of feeling. Both their camaraderie and Kirk's pain at Edith's demise is superbly evoked. This show grips the emotions as few others do while at the same time pushing for peace (albeit at the right times), love, helping others and understanding. This isn't just the best episode of *Star Trek*, it's one of the best episodes ever produced on any episodic television show. Of course, the show won the Hugo Award, but it's hard to imagine it losing an Emmy except that *Star Trek* was a show with a limited audience and had yet to reach the mythic proportions it does today.

"Amok Time" came next, the second season premiere and another very good episode. Sex is always a delicate subject on television and it's amazing that the sexual life of a Vulcan could even be discussed at all. Ted Sturgeon claimed that at his polite insistence, the line "Having is not as fine a thing as wanting" was saved. The Kirk-Spock battle is energetic and exciting, particularly when this episode was first aired. Arlene Martel, who had appeared in the "Demon With A Glass Hand" episode of *The Outer Limits*, is fine as a beautiful, coldly logical Vulcan. Celia Lovsky, Peter Lorre's first wife, made an excellent Vulcan matriarch.

Pevney's next two efforts, "The Apple" and "Catspaw," had inferior scripts and consequently were not very good, but

Pevney was back in form with "Journey To Babel." Like "Balance of Terror," this episode was very effective due to the number of conflicts and problems which hook the viewer's interest. The emotional interplay between Spock and his parents is particularly intriguing, especially in what it reveals to us about Spock and Vulcans in general. This show is also good at communicating that the Federation is not entirely human-dominated, and that the tactics of diplomacy are as tricky as ever. That fact is also true in Pevney's "Friday's Child." His direction quickly underlines the antagonism between the groups on Capella IV. Eleen's snobbery is appropriately displayed and annoying, leading to McCoy's memorable "I'm a doctor, not an escalator" line. The Klingons are portrayed as incredibly foolhardy.

"The Deadly Years," where Kirk, Spock, McCoy, Scotty and Galway grow older, probably served as the basis for the animated episodes "The Terratine Incident" where they grow smaller, "The Ambergris Element" where Kirk and Spock are turned into water-breathers (although it's also very similar to a 1936 Flash Gordon plot), and especially "The Counterclock Incident" where the crew grows younger. "The Deadly Years" reprises the Corbomite Maneuver and is generally quite average, as is "Wolf In The Fold" where the spirit of Jack the Ripper invades the Enterprise. The "She's dead, Jim!" got its greatest working out here. "The Immunity Syndrome" was likewise an average episode with the ridiculous notion of a planet-sized one-celled animal being brought colorfully to life.

Pevney's direction of "The Trouble With Tribbles" however does show his flair for comic timing. Each actor brings off David Gerrold's jokes and Pevney quickly moves along to the next. The bar fight is well-staged, although of short duration. William Campbell's despicable unctuousness is delightfully played upon. The most effective choice in the episode was the hanging of an AMT Enterprise model outside of a K-7 window. Whit Bissel, William Schallert and the late Stanley Adams all turn in fine performances under Pevney's direction.

Ralph Senensky has done his best television work outside of *Star Trek* with such episodes as "My Name Is Martin Burnham" (*Arrest and Trial*), "Printer's Devil" (with Burgess Meredith from the Charles Beaumont story for *Twilight Zone*), "The Train" (for *Mission: Impossible*), "Night of the Big Blast" (*Wild Wild West*), *The Family Nobody Wanted* (tv movie), "The Grandchild" (*The Waltons*) and especially "The Sound of Sunlight" (*Westside Medical*).

Except for "The Paradise Syndrome" and Murray Golden's handling of "Requiem for Methuselah," Senensky did the best third season episodes—"Is There In Truth No Beauty?" and "The Tholian Web." "The Tholian Web" is best remembered for its spectacular (for sixties television) special effects, the tension created in its quasi-ghost story and for Kirk's being deprived of speech for a significant portion of the episode. "Is There In Truth No Beauty?" is definitely and peculiarly science fiction. Kollos the Medusan is utterly alien and remains so. However, his sense of wonder when he inhabits Spock's body is quite well done (quoting Shakespeare's line "O Brave New World that contains wonders such as these" from *The Tempest*). Miranda is obviously named after the character in the same play, and Diana Muldaur (who would go on to play Doctor Pulaski during the second season of *Star Trek: The Next Generation*) does a good job as a handicapped, jealous but sympathetic person. Spock's madness is a bit dramatically contrived but, unfortunately, this is nothing new.

Senensky's other *Star Trek* work, "This Side of Paradise," "Metamorphosis," "Obsession" and "Return To Tomorrow" are all likewise above average. It is interesting to note that there is an alien/human love affair in both "Beauty" and "Metamorphosis", and alien minds taking over human bodies in both "Return To Tomorrow" and "Beauty." This suggests some thematic concerns. The alien spore lures people into forsaking their responsibilities in "This Side of Paradise," which allows Spock to love for the first time, but which would spell disaster for the Enterprise crew if they cannot combat the spores' influence. The episode manages to be happy, carefree and touching, but its message is clearly and importantly stated. The love story in "Metamorphosis" is quite touching and the love between Sargon and his wife, Thalassa, in "Return To Tomorrow" argues that love is a universal emotion, regardless of race—alien or humanoid. "Obsession" has another cloud creature, this one of a blood-sucking nature and Kirk's ability to be obsessed is clearly shown (as if we didn't know already.) We do glimpse the torture of self-doubt that Kirk must rigidly keep under control. In *Star Trek: The Motion Picture*, Kirk was likewise obsessed with getting the Enterprise into a fight with another dangerous cloud from outer space. In *The Wrath of Khan* we see more of his self-doubt as well as his coming to grips with defeat as he must accept Spock's death. Senensky also directed "Bread And Circuses." None of Senensky's work is outstanding, but none of it is below par either. He is a dependable craftsman.

Jud Taylor, however, is not. With the notable exception of "The Paradise Syndrome," all of Taylor's *Star Trek*'s were badly directed. ("Wink Of An Eye," "Let That Be Your Last Battlefield," "Mark of Gideon" and "The Cloud Minders"). Despite the cliches, "The Paradise Syndrome" does manage to be both pleasant and idyllic, but Taylor's other work is far more heavy-handed. An example of his amateurishness is his zooming in and out on a blinking klaxon to try to generate excitement in "Let That Be Your Last Battlefield." Thankfully his work improved by the time he did *Tail Gunner Joe, Return to Earth* (with Cliff Robertson as Buzz Aldrin) and *Future Cop* (which ripped off Harlan Ellison and Ben Bova's story "Brillo," and for which they received a hefty settlement).

Marvin Chomsky started his television career directing the "Night Of The Iron Fist," "Night Of The Vipers," and "Night Of The Undead" episodes for *Wild, Wild West*. He has also directed the pilot for Bill Bixby's *The Magician* series, parts 3, 4 and 6 of *Roots* and all of *Holocaust*, which shows that he can be a good director when he tried.

When he worked on *Star Trek* he obviously was not trying. His direction of "And The Children Shall Lead," "Day

Of The Dove" and "All Our Yesterdays" is quite bad. "Day Of The Dove" is one of the better third season episodes, due largely to Jerome Bixby's script and Michael Ansara's performance as Kang, but the direction is awkward and clumsy throughout. "All Our Yesterdays" is somewhat popular, probably due to the appeal of an uninhibited Spock for the female fans, but it is nonetheless quite bad. Mr. Atoz, the librarian, stands for "A to Z" which shows you how ridiculous this episode gets. There is no logical reason for Spock's regression, Kirk's falling through the time portal is quite arbitrary and the whole thing looks quite cheap. The less said about "And The Children Shall Lead," voted the single worst episode of the show, the better.

This, for the most part, concludes our discussion of *Star Trek* directors as I have very little information on such as Robert Sparr ("Shore Leave"), James Komack ("A Piece Of The Action"), John Meredith Lucas ("The Ultimate Computer," "The Enterprise Incident," "Elaan Of Troyius), John Erman ("The Empath"), Herb Wallerstein ("That Which Survives," "Whom Gods Destroy," "Turnabout Intruder"), David Alexander ("Plato's Stepchildren," "The Way To Eden") and Herb Kenwith "The Lights Of Zetar").

For others, *Star Trek* was just a minor footnote in their careers: Harvey Hart ("Mudd's Women"), Robert Gist ("The Galileo Seven"), Don McDougall ("The Squire Of Gothos"), Michael O'Herlihy ("Tomorrow Is Yesterday"), John Newland ("Errand Of Mercy"), Herschel Daugherty ("The Gamesters Of Triskelion") and Anton "Tony" Leader ("For The World Is Hollow And I Have Touched The Sky").

Needless to say, some directors did their best and some did less, but *Star Trek* used a fine pool of directorial talent from experienced hands like Oswald and Pevney to future very successful directors like Sargent, McEveety and Gist. They were all fortunate to have a fine cast and crew of the Enterprise to work with, and the resulting episodes were some of the sixties' best television, containing qualities that are often missing in the medium today.

Television is a less personal, more rushed medium than film, and consequently these artists and craftsmen frequently do not get the recognition they deserve. There is no doub their efforts have proved fruitful in making *Star Trek* one of the best loved,series of all time.

The same fan, Allen Koszowski's rendition of the third member of STAR TREK's unique triad. Dr. Leonard "Bones" McCoy added emotion to the mix, balancing Spock's logic. Captain Kirk provided the center of stabilization, always taking both viewpoints into account before rendering the final decision.

This attractive actress and veteran of STAR TREK produced a poster of herself a few years ago so racy it was reviewed in Playboy.

Angelique Pettyjohn

by James Van Hise

Angelique Pettyjohn appeared as Shahna, the Drill Thrall, in the Star Trek episode "The Gamesters of Triskelion."

EI:

How were you chosen for that role and what was it like working on that episode of *Trek*?

PETTYJOHN:

I had a background as a theatre arts major in college—high school drama and all of those sorts of things, like acting classes. I worked as a professional dancer in Las Vegas for a while and then I came to Hollywood and started working as an actress. I had a small part here, and then a larger part there. It was about three years into my career, when I had done a number of different films and was a working actress in Hollywood. My agent, as agents do, got the script for that particular week of *Star Trek*. He read through it and saw a part with a description that he felt suited me, so he sent me in for an interview.

When you go in for an interview for a part, you're in an outer office. A secretary gives you a script which has the description of the character you're to play and some dialogue, and you have

about ten minutes to look through it. Then you go into an inner office where you have a casting director, the director, the producer and various people. Then you'll sit there and you'll read it. It's called a cold reading. I was sitting there in the outer office reading the character description which said: "A green-haired, green-eyed Amazon leaps from behind a rock, pinning Shatner with a spear."

I thought about. When I went in for the interview the first thing I said was, "Gentlemen, before I waste my time and yours, I really don't feel I fit the description of this character."

They asked "Well, why not?"

I said, "Well, I've got the green eyes and I'm sure you can fix me up with green hair, but I'm hardly an Amazon. I'm only five foot six."

They laughed and they said, "Look, honey, next to Shatner, you'll look like an Amazon. Go ahead and read the script."

I didn't realize that he's a shorter man because he looks so big on screen. So I read the script.

I always wore bangs because I have a very high forehead. They asked me to pull the hair away from my forehead

29

for a minute and I said, "No, no, I don't look good that way." They said, "Please," and so I pulled the hair back from my forehead and they asked me to wait in the outer office for a minute.

It usually doesn't work like that in a part. You usually have to wait several days and then they call you back. I went into the outer office and sat there for about fifteen minutes. Evidently they called my agent and then called me back in and said, "You're hired, go to wardrobe." It was that quick.

That was how I got it. I got my script and we had several rehearsals before we started shooting. These were with the stunt coordinator. If you watch that particular episode, "The Gamesters of Triskelion," you'll see a man in blue that fights with Shatner near the end. The man with the blue skin was actually the stunt coordinator for all the *Star Trek* episodes. He handled the stuntwork and taught us the fighting with the poles. He choreographed the fight scenes. So we had a couple days of rehearsal with the stunt coordinator before we started filming.

EI:

What was it like actually doing the show since much more than action scenes were involved?

PETTYJOHN:

At first it was really delightful because I found Shatner to be friendly, gregarious, rather mischievous with a twinkling-eyed little smile, a really marvelous person around the set, and comfortable to be around. He made me feel very comfortable. At first, when I came in, I was very much in awe of working with him. I was a little bit up-tight around him, but he made me instantly feel very comfortable, like a friend and fellow actress. He wasn't pretentious at all, but was very friendly.

I thought Leonard Nimoy was marvelous, intelligent, quiet, and a very polite man. I respected him very much.

I loved Nichelle Nichols. I thought she was just a doll. We got to be good friends on the set and after I finished shooting I saw her on a personal basis a couple of times.

Walter Koenig was a really nice guy. Very nice. Very friendly. Rather quiet. He seemed to be a little on the shy side.

I loved the shooting. Just before we finished shooting that particular episode, three or four days after we started filming it, the producer came in. Now this was before the marches and everybody changed things around. The producer came in during lunch time and made an announcement to the cast and crew. He was sorry to say the network had cancelled the series. Everyone was very depressed. The last two days of shooting everyone was kind of down around the set because of that and because they all loved working together so much. On my last day of shooting, I had a particular speech where I said, "Good-bye, Jim Kirk, I will watch the lights in the sky and remember." I had tears in my eyes and those tears were real because I was thinking, as my motivation as an actress, that it was good-bye to *Star Trek*. I watch the film and the lights in the sky and remember this experience. It meant a great deal to me. I really cried and that's how I meant it because I knew that the series wasn't going to be shooting anymore.

Later on, I understand, many fans got together, wrote letters, marched on the network and it stayed on for another season. After that, it was cancelled. At that time, that was my experience during the week of shooting.

EI:

Was the collar you wore wired?

PETTYJOHN:

The original collar in the fight scenes was not wired. It was just something that you wear like an ornament. In close-ups, where the colors were to go on and light up, we had a wire running from the collar. It was taped to the body and down the back, down a leg and to the floor and along the floor. We had to make sure no matter how much we moved we kept one foot on the floor so we didn't tear up the wire. Then there was a man who was off-camera who watched. At a cue from the director he hit a switch and turned the power on. We began agonizing or choking or whatever it was the collars were supposed to be doing to us. That's how that operated.

I have one that was made for me by one of the wonderful *Star Trek* fans that I've met since I did the episode, and this one has a battery pack in it.

EI:

Have you been to any other conventions prior to the current one here in Los Angeles?

PETTYJOHN:

I've been to two others, one in New York about three or four years ago. It was a huge convention with about eight thousand people. I really enjoyed it. I felt like a Rock star. I needed several

security guards there because there were just so many people. I did a guest appearance consisting of a ten minute Jazz dance number with music and slides and all kinds of things to create a mood. Then afterwards I did questions and answers with the audience. I didn't have my posters at the time but that's what gave me the idea for the posters. I met so many wonderful fans who wanted photographs of me and at the time I didn't even have any 8 x 10 glossies from *Star Trek*. I had duplicated the costume before the convention and some fans had duplicated some of the other pieces for me. I had a photographer of mine from Las Vegas, who's also a *Playboy* photographer, take new photographs of me as the *Star Trek* character Shahna to publish as posters.

EI:

What other productions have you been in?

PETTYJOHN:

There were so many that it's difficult to recal. I did a movie called *The Mad Doctor Of Blood Island* which was released on TV as *The Tomb Of The Living Dead*. I did a Western with Glenn Ford called *Heaven With A Gun*. I was in *The President's Analyst*. I did a motorcycle picture for AIP called *Hell's Bells*. I was in an Elvis Presley picture called *Clambake* and in *Rough Night In Jericho* with Dean Martin. For television, I was on *Get Smart Batman, Girl From Uncle* (where I had a fairly large part), *Felony Squad, Good Morning World* and a number of others. There's a long list but those are the ones that come into memory very quickly.

Here's a compilation of notable quotes uttered by various sources after viewing Star Trek over the last two decades.

What They're Saying About Star Trek

compiled by Al Christensen

". . .*Star Trek* (1968), after beginning well with a cleverly constructed double episode called 'Menagerie', degenerated sharply into stock situations. 'Menagerie' is an interesting example of prudent TV production. Originally made as 'The Cage', a one-hour pilot for the series, it starred Jeffrey Hunter as the captain of a space battleship who rescues castaway Susan Oliver from telepathic aliens on a dying world. By the time the series had been accepted. Hunter was no longer available, so the producers incorporated the original hour into a two hour programme in which William Shatner, the series' original star, investigates the circumstances of Hunters landing, with Hunter, a disfigured and unrecognizable victim of a space accident, beside him on the ship. The first programme was viewed in segments as a flashback, some extra action added to tie up loose ends. On the whole an extremely clever piece of reorganization.

"Like so many other series, *Star Trek* became caught in a profitable groove, in its case the idea of worlds in which societies had developed parallel with earth. This preoccupation began with 'Tomorrow is Yesterday', an early episode in which Shatner's future starship is sent back in time, landing on the Earth of the Sixties. Presumably intoxicated by the ease of doing an sf show in stock sets and with formula situations, the producers soon offered a planet like Nazi Germany, another like Chicago in the Thirties. A third story was nothing but a space version of a wartime submarine drama, two space ships hunting each other with sophisticated versions of sonar. Marginally interesting as esoterica, none of these programmes deserve serious consideration as sf.

"An exception, however, was an episode called 'Charlie X' , directed by Lawrence Dobkin with Robert Walker Jr. as a telepath which the starship Enterprise unwittingly picks up. Adolescent and vindictive, the boy slips from puppy love to childish hatred in a moment, while the crew's reactions convey perfectly the terror of men faced with a power impossible to fight. Walker's acting is superb, an animal contortion of his face horribly suggesting the blast of hate that destroys those who oppose him. With it he melts the pieces of a three-dimensional chess set on which he has lost the game, and later, being angered by the laughter of some crewman, stops them abruptly. Seen first only as shadows, a girl gropes around the corner of a corridor to reveal her face changed to a smooth mask of flesh. Shape means nothing in his world, and when he changes a girl into a scuttling lizard we imagine when he advances on another with his hand behind his back and the coy offer of 'something for her' that it is this creature he will flourish in her face. But his hand holds instead a rose. Horror too can have its poetry, evil its own special beauty."

JOHN BAXTER, Science Fiction in the Cinema.

Paperback Library, copyright 1970

". . .This is now diagnosable as the *Star Trek* syndrome. As science fiction goes, *Star Trek* isn't much. There's not a fresh idea in all the three years of it put together, nothing that has not been done before, and is usually much better in the pages of some science fiction magazine or book. But the people who saw *Star Trek* numbered forty million. The overwhelming majority of them had never been exposed to anything like it before. They had never really thought about the possibility of life on other planets, or time travel, or what it would be like to cruise through space, or how societies might resemble (or differ from) our own, until they caught it on the boob tube, and to them it was Revelation. To them. To us, decades earlier. Above all, to me."

-FREDERICK POHL, 'The way future was.'

Ballantine Books, copyright 1978.

". . . Yet I remember that *Star Trek* was supposed to have some vast effect on the circulation of science fiction. Probably it had some but not much. And when Sputnik went up, everyone was convinced that the age of science fiction had begun -after which the circulation of the magazines continued to fall slightly.

"Obviously, only time will provide the answers. But in my opinion, *Star Wars* is going to have a very strong effect on the continued success of science fiction.

"I discount results of *Star Trek* from my experience with the followers of that television program. By and large, the audience that watched those programs did not become fans of science fiction, though there was considerable science fiction used. They became primarily fans of Mr. Spock, the long-eared Vulcan member of the crew, as played by Leonard Nimoy -and to a lesser extent of the rest of the crew. It was much more like other fandoms than like the fandom of science fiction. Many, in fact, acted as if they believed in the literal truth of what they saw, and most seemed to take the program far too seriously to dabble around with anything else in science fiction. . .

". . . But *Star Wars* has a different impact. To begin with, of course, it is science fiction from start to finish. It takes robots, its aliens, its star travel and everything else very much for granted, just as science fiction learned to do. (George Lucas, unlike most Hollywood directors, seems to have an excellent familiarity with science fiction.) The characters are not the basic center of interest -rather the whole movie is.

"Furthermore, there is a much stronger tie-in with paperback science fiction. Ballantine/Del Rey Books is bringing out a series of 'spin-off' novels, each dealing with some of the characters of the movie. These will be by established science fiction authors. It is hoped that readers who buy such books will be led to other works by those same authors, thus moving them from STAR WARS to general science fiction. The first of all these books, SPLINTER OF THE MINDS EYE by Alan Dean Foster, has already been released, and preliminary reports following a healthy sale indicate that Foster's other books are beginning to sell more rapidly.

"In the case of *Star Trek*, the original novelizations were done by James Blish, a highly regarded writer; but when the young fans of the series tried his other books, they must have found them totally beyond their age level. There was little cross-movement into science fiction."

-LESTER DEL REY, 'The World of Science Fiction.'

Ballantine Books, Copyright 1979.

". . . We chose the Chief Engineer, largely because in the contemporary world it is a fact that a vastly disproportionate number of ships engineers are Scots, and that seemed a reasonable thing to project into the future.

"Alas, some critics have resented that, and a few have accused us of stealing Mr. Sinclair from *Star Trek*. We didn't. Mr Sinclair is what he is for perfectly sound astrographical reasons."

-JERRY POURNELLE

(Discussing a character from a book he co-authored with LARRY NIVEN, 'A Mote in God's Eye'),

'A Step Farther Out' Ace Books, Copyright 1979.

". . . I have the same trouble with *Star Trek*, which I know has a wide following and which some thoughtful friends tell me I should view allegorically and not literally. But when astronauts from Earth set down on some far distant planet and find the human beings there in the midst of a conflict between two nuclear super powers, which call themselves the Yangs and the Coms, or their phonetic equivalents, the suspension of disbelief crumbles. In a global terrestrial society centuries in the future, the ship's officers are embarrassingly Anglo-American. Only two of twelve or fifteen interstellar vessels are given non-English names, Kongo and Potemkin. (Potemkin and not Aurora?) And the idea of a successful cross between a 'Vulcan' and a terrestrial simply ignores what we know of molecular biology. (As I have remarked elsewhere, such a cross is about as likely as the successful mating of a man and a petunia.) According to Harlan Ellison, even such sedate biological novelties as Mr. Spock's pointy ears and permanently querulous eyebrows were considered by network executives far too daring; such enormous differences between Vulcans and humans would only confuse the audience, they thought, and a move was made to have all physiologically distinguishing Vulcan features effaced."

CARL SAGAN, Broca's Brain.

Random House. Copyright 1974

"... A feature film? Good idea; so Paramount started preparing scripts and lining up talent. The talent was coy. Shatner, Nimoy and all the others had been convinced of their godhood by tens of thousands of Trekkies at dozens of conventions, and each one expected to see that reflected in a pay check. A script was also elusive. First shot went to Roddenberry himself, who created a sort of 'generations' story of the old age of the crew, coming back for for one last go at the bad guys. Paramount nixed it and went on. It all took time, but as months passed they had a script at last. Philip Kaufman was signed to direct what he called 'essentially a Leonard Nimoy Spock story. . . it was a love story and it was adult science fiction' when the axe fell.

"... The fourth network dream died hard, but at last it died and Paramount made its bet. It would be a feature film. Only question was, what would the film be? Roddenberry wrote the script, and the Paramount people vetoed it. They hired Robert Silverberg to write one, and vetoed that too. At least a dozen writers of one kind or another were put on the payroll for long periods or short to try and come up with the magic idea that would make it all come together. But none of the writers could please; and at last Paramount remembered the scripts it had commissioned for the 'Fourth Network ' series. It reached back in among them and pulled out the Alan Dean Foster story that had been intended as a lead off. And that became *Star Trek: The Motion Picture*. Viewers who think that TMP seems rather like any random episode from the television series have exactly the right of it.

"There exists a novel version of the script, written be Gene Roddenberry, which shows a lot of inventiveness and interesting detail. Very little of it appears in the film. It is not likely that Roddenberry chose to eliminate the scenes, or that Paramount refused to foot the bill. The explanation is almost certainly that the special effects fiasco which almost doomed the film caused them to be dropped, for at almost the last minute Paramount switched special effects studios and turned everything over to Douglas Trumbull when the original contractor failed to deliver.

"*Star Trek: The Motion Picture* represents Hollywood at its lunatic worst. What appeared on the screen was no more than a rescue operation, the best compromise that could be reached between what Roddenberry wanted and what cold reality allowed. And yet-what a pleasure to see them together again!"

FREDERIK POHL and FREDERIK POHL IV,

'Science Fiction studies in Film.

Ace Books, Copyright 1981.

Editor's note: It's interesting how Frederick Pohl's opinion of STAR TREK seemed to change from the quote published in 1978 to the one taken from 1981.

A once in a lifetime opportunity occurred when Star Trek: The Motion Picture was filmed—fans were invited to be part of a major sequence in the movie!

Part Of The Magic

by Dennis Fischer

"The good thing about doing a film is that now for the first time we can have a visual perspective you can't get in television. We'll see the tremendous size of the Enterprise. And in the series where they said there were 430 crew members, we're going to show them all."

—ROBERT WISE

Ever had a dream come true? Ever had an extraordinary piece of good fortune fall right into your lap? Well, this happened to me one evening while attending a meeting of LASFS* (The Los Angeles Science Fantasy Society). I had been talking to a man in a *Star Trek: The Motion Picture* T-shirt, and he had been telling me about working on the special effects for the film. I found out what I could and went over to re-enter the LASFS clubhouse when Leigh Strother-Vien, a tall, good-looking science fiction fan, walked up to me and said, "How would you like to be an extra in the *Star Trek* movie?" While I do not recall my jaw dropping to my feet, it would have been appropriate. In a daze I asked for further details. Apparently, while visiting Bjo Trimble's** house, Bjo had asked Leigh if she would like to be in the *Star Trek* movie and would she find other

fans who might be interested. Leigh said, "SURE!!!" and so now it was my turn to be asked the same question. Rest assured, my response was no different. If this was a dream, I didn't want to wake up.

I was told that the *Star Trek* casting crew wanted people between the ages of 20 and 40; men ranging in height from 5'8" to 6'2", sizes 40-42; and women ranging from 5'6" to 5'8" wearing sizes 8-10. They wanted us for two days, and they wanted as many fans as possible as a way of thanking the fans for their efforts and perseverance. All I had to do was to call up Bjo and get my name up on the list for the casting call.

There was just one problem. At that time I was the right size, but I was just under 20 and just over 6'2". (I'm 6'4", actually.) I can remember back when I was 13 years old and I had just read *The Making of Star Trek* by Stephen E. Whitfield and Gene Roddenberry. I dreamt about somehow becoming "part of the magic" — that wonderful movie-making process. I daydreamed about being an extra, and then I read about two people being dismissed as extras because they had been too tall. Being inclined to be more on the tall side than on the lucky side, I feared that this would happen to me even if I got the chance, but of course now that the chance had come along, I was not going to give up without trying.

"Who am I anyway? / Am I my resume'?

That is a picture of a person I don't know.

What does he want of me?

What shall I try to be? / So many faces

all around me and here we go . . . / I need

this job,/ Oh God, I need this show."
— Paul in A CHORUS LINE

Anyone who has been through a musical's cattle call knows somewhat what I went through next. The audition was held on October 9, 1978 at Paramount Studios by the old Gower Gate. I stood on line outside the gate with Don Fanning and Marlene Willauer, two good friends from Icarus, UCLA's science fiction club. While we were waiting, we conversed with Mike Hodel, who at the time was the host of "Hour 25," a science fiction radio show which airs Friday nights at ten on KPFK in Los Angeles. The guard started reading names off the list, and it wasn't long before our names were called. We entered the gate and Bjo escorted us to the soundstage, pointing the sights out along the way. "That is a soundstage. This is a hole in the road. Any questions? I've only been doing this job for the last half hour." I answered in my best naive voice, "Gosh, it looks just like it does in the movies!"

Upon entering the soundstage, we were given a handout written by Gene Roddenberry thanking us for our participation. What was needed was 170 men and 20 women to fill the remaining unfilled costumes. The costumes had been premade, but the Screen Extras Guild (SEG) had been unable to fill the uniforms with enough people of the proper dimensions, so now the fans were given their chance along with any Guild members who had missed the Guild audition call. About 300 men and 60 women had shown up.

The selection process was exceedingly cold and impersonal. A group was brought down and looked over by wardrobe people, and they quickly weeded out those who would obviously not fit into the costumes. It is an unfortunate fact of life that many loyal *Star Trek* fans do not fit the narrow restrictions placed on size, so they had to be coldly turned down. Those who remained were ushered into an adjoining area which contained Robin Williams' dressing room, to await others who made it through the semi-final preliminaries. Some were instantly selected to be aliens. After this was done, the semi-finalists were trotted out again to have the film's director, Robert Wise, make the final selection. Since the women went first, Don and I watched as Robert gestured Marlene to come forward and another girl named Joanna Christy. He looked from one girl to another and settled on Joanna. Marlene went back into line only to be selected later.

We learned the significance of the selection later. Apparently Mr. Wise had been looking for potential female Vulcans. Joanna reportedly did come to earth for awhile after the selection, but wandered around muttering, "I'm a

Vulcan. I'm a Vulcan." Friends worried about her being stopped by a traffic cop and informing the officer that she was a Vulcan, decided to drive her home that night. Meanwhile, Don was selected to be a "big headed alien." I waited my turn near John Watts and Jay Smith. John was selected to be an Andorian, and Jay chuckled. For three straight years, John had gone to Bjo's Equicons dressed as one sort of blue-skinned character or another. Finally, Robert Wise walked by where I was striking my best "Star Fleet cadet" pose. He jerked his thumb over his shoulder, and I was in!

With each selection, the fans offered a round of applause, which really puzzled the old time Guild members. When you work at being an extra for a living, each selection means one less chance for you to have a job, so there was no figuring out these crazy *Star Trek* fans. Even when they didn't make it, they hung around and applauded their friends and others.

All there was left to do that evening was to make an appointment for a fitting. I talked with some fans who had accompanied a friend down to the audition and had been able to audition themselves when they let everybody in. Their friend didn't make it, but they did. We were all shown the *Star Trek* haircut that we would have to have. It was pretty much the old haircut with short hair and pointed sideburns. The person next to me groaned when he realized that he would have to trim his carefully groomed mustache. He was Walt Doty, a handsome young student from USC and co-president of the ASTRA Science Fiction Club.

We found out why Gene Roddenberry

hadn't shown up that evening. He was out having dinner rather than having to face any broken-hearted but unsuitable *Star Trek* fan. He was worried that he would go soft and say, "Well, she's done a lot of work as a fan for the show's return. Couldn't we make an exception in this case?" Unfortunately, he could not allow for the number of possible exceptions likely to turn up. We all remain grateful to the man.

Outside the soundstage, and after a quick rendition of "We're off to see the Wizard," Don, Marlene and I joined Leigh and Alan Frisbie outside the studio. We decided to celebrate by going to a Bagel Nosh. Alan informed us that he had been selected as an "alternate." "What does that mean?" asked Leigh. Alan sighed, "That means I only have to kill 15 people."

"Come on and dress me, dress me, dress me,

in my finest array.

Come on dress me, dress me, dress me,

today is doe-me-doe day."

—Dr. T from THE 5000 FINGERS OF DR. T

It was only a few days later that Don and I checked in at the Paramount front gate to get in for our fitting. We wandered over to stage seventeen where the men were being outfitted. There were parts of sets from the film there. One part looked like someone's personal transporter. On the inside it was very smooth and streamlined, but the outside looked like that of any other set's. Another set piece resembled the Moonbase Alpha shuttle. Behind a partition were the uniforms. I walked up to the person who was obviously in charge, but he was busy helping out a mis-directed individual. (The guy was sup-posed to be outfitted as a Vulcan priest and this area only contained crew-member uniforms.) Finally someone got around to me. "Here, try this one on." It was a brown jumpsuit several sizes too big. "It fits. Let's get you some shoes." Thankfully they did not have any of the extremely un-comfortable scuba shoes in my size, so I settled on a pair of tennis shoes cov-ered with brown material which matched my uniform. I was all set! Now, for the big day. . .

"Looks like we made it!"
— Grace Lee Whitney

On the big day I got up at 5: 30, had a shower and waited impatiently for Don and Marlene to show up. We arrived at the studio promptly at 7:00 A.M., and were quickly admitted. Marlene went off to Stage Two, the ladies dressing rooms, while Don and I went back to Stage 17. It did not take long to don my apparel, but then the waiting started as others arrived to be suited up. I walked around endeavoring to question those that were suiting up some 300 extras.

The basic costume colors were beige, grey-blue, brown and white. There was also a hydroponics farmer/recreation outfit with a loose open shirt. To find out what branch of the service a person was in, one had to look at their em-blem. Green meant that they belonged to the medical services; orange in-dicated sciences; gold was command; yellow for communications; and white or silver were for the general services people. (Well, someone has to swab the decks and wash the uniforms or, at least, push the buttons on the machines which do.) On a shoulder stripe, a tri-angle was placed if you were an ensign, or a gold bar/thread if you were an en-sign, or a gold bar/thread if you were a lieutenant, and the uniform had special raised portions across the chest and the standard sleeve stripes if you were a higher ranking officer. I had a green emblem and no defined rank. Oh, well, as a cadet in the medical services, I was probably an orderly.

Makeup was starting for those who needed it. I looked briefly at the portion of the transporter which was on the soundstage. Underneath an operating instructions sign were instructions—in nonsense Latin! Oh well, at a distance it looked very convincing. I went around the set to be checked out by makeup. Makeup decided that my hair-cut had not been enough and proceeded to make amends. They also pointed and almost eliminated my sideburns. They didn't take long as there were many people yet to go.

For the aliens, the simplest were the "Deltans." These would be composed of anyone who happened to be bald. Don as a 'big head' had a methane mask with light up eyes covering his face. The back of his head looked like someone's posterior. The Vulcans were done with pointed ears and yellowish skin. For some reason, only dark-haired, brown-eyed people were con-sidered as Vulcans, which lead one fan to complain why there couldn't be any blue-eyed Vulcans? There was a blue-skinned Andorian, who must have had blue in his genes. There were bump-heads who resembled Frankenstein's monster with long blonde hair, and they looked like they were ready to do the "Time Warp." There were purple Gorn-like lizards, and another purple alien that resembled the mutant from *This Island Earth*, but with a smaller cranium. My favorite makeup though was done by Paula Crist. To me she looked like a female Tellerite, but she informed me that actually she was a Czintii. (No relation to Larry Niven's Kzin.)

The waiting continued, but was made more pleasant by the fact that the women began joining the men, and coffee and tea were served. There was a small incident, though. A Screen Extras Guild member was passing out literature de-nouncing the use of waivers on this or any project. This left some fans hurt and confused. After all, if it had not been for their efforts there never would have been a *Star Trek* movie.

Kathleen Sky, author of the book *Vulcan*, and David Gerrold, looked over the handout and criticized the poor writing technique. It was easy to pass on to more pleasant subjects. Kathleen announced that she had just sold her science fiction epic, *Shalom!*, to Bantam books; now she just had to write the book. David talked about writing a humorous *Star Trek* novel, the un-pleasant experience as story editor on the *Buck Rogers* tv series, and visiting the Heinleins. It had been four hours since we arrived before we were finally asked to proceed to the soundstage.

We slowly filed into the enormous set of the recreation room. Behind us through the "viewing screens" we could see one of the Enterprise nacelle pylons towering behind us, and part of the "dry dock." Laid into the orange carpet were small pits where electronic games could be played. The assistants ushered people into places as quickly as possible, trying to close up the gaps. Some of the fans started to pretend to play one of the electronic games, be-fuddling some of the on lookers trying to figure out how it worked.

Being tall, taller than the principals in fact, meant that I had to stand near the back of this large group of people, but far be it for me to complain. I was just glad to be there at all. I ended up stand-ing between Katherine Kurtz, a tall blonde lady who is the author of the "Deryni" series, and Leigh Strother-Vien, the red-headed aforementioned LASFS member who got me into this in the first place. Don in his "big head" costume was just to her right, while Walt Doty was located in a group of other blacks. Poor Bjo ended up to my left behind two very tall people. David Gerrold was positioned near the front, while Kathleen Sky and Jay Smith formed a couple behind us. On the bal-cony were Vincent, a guy in a purple lizard outfit who found he could stick his tongue out of his plastic mouth, and James T. Kirk, a fan who had his name legally changed to that of some famous starship captain. Then there was Mar-lene, who hobnobbed with Susan Sack-ett, Louise Stange, Michelle and Mrs. Wise. The last were, along with Bjo, the only ladies under 5'6" allowed. They all had specially made white uni-forms. Louise was the president of the Leonard Nimoy Fan Club (LNFC), and Leonard had made a special request for her inclusion. Michelle worked in Gene

Roddenberry's office and she jokingly told everyone that she had threatened to refile everything if she got left out.

Robert Wise came up and told everyone to memorize their places. He looked to see how the scene would appear on screen. He decided that he didn't like the gaps created by the pits where the electronic games were, so we broke for lunch while the pits were covered over. Unfortunately, the yellow communicator I had could not be used to order food to be beamed over to me so. . . obviously I had to go to the food. The communicator was oversized and tended to slip, but nonetheless I had one.

Waiting in line for lunch, I found out that the men weren't the only ones with hair problem. With the exception of the Indian crewmembers who kept their traditional haircuts and jewelry, none of the other women were allowed to have long hair. This meant that it either had to be slicked down or done up in a bun. Also, the fact that no glasses were allowed was a disadvantage to some (including me).

At least the crewmembers of the Enterprise ate well. We were served steaks on the soundstage where THE CLONE MASTER had been filmed some time before. The crewmembers relaxed and talked with one another.

Marlene: "You're enjoying this."

David Gerrold: "I do this every month."

Marlene: "What do you do on the Enterprise?"

David Gerrold: "Disciplinary measures."

Marlene: "Whips and chains?"

David Gerrold: "Right!"

One thing about David Gerrold's uniform. Unlike my somewhat baggy one, his was skin tight. Many of the uniforms were filled with elastic which made them look good, but they were uncomfortable to wear. Some people were afraid to bend over for fear that they would be snapped back. The costumes for the females were made for extremely short-waisted people, which was a drawback. Also, the bosoms were made somewhat larger than average, so some women had to resort to the Kleenex method of filling out what wasn't there. Once in these, they were hard to get out of. David Gerrold announced that he had to go to the bathroom and needed help getting out of his uniform. Several females volunteered. "That wasn't exactly what I had in mind," said David, reluctantly turning them down.

On the way out I stopped by Grace Lee Whitney's dressing room. Her son had first been an extra in the episode "Miri," and now he was back as a full grown Vulcan. I had talked with Grace a few years earlier about whether she was going to be in the long announced *Star Trek* movie. At that point she had not been asked. She said she had enjoyed her first half season on *Star Trek*, but she had been let go because someone at the network thought that Kirk should have a new girlfriend every week. (To quote Shatner: "He uses up the old one!") Grace had indicated then that she was tired of Paramount leading the fans on about the *Star Trek* film for so long to milk what money they could out of continued syndication sales and toy sales. (This lead one of Roddenberry's secretaries to wear a shirt that read: "Paramount is a Klingon agent!") She also asked fans that liked her to request that she be in the movie if it ever happened. Here we were together at last, and it was happening!

I returned to soundstage 17 to find that Walter Koenig had dropped by with his family. He had planned to give his family a tour of the sets, but security was so tight they would not even allow him through. I compared communicators. His had a mother-of-pearl finish, but otherwise was quite similar. Some portions of the sets were accessible. I toured a large decompression chamber, a section of corridor, a section of the hydroponics lab, and saw some cryogenics chambers. They each had "Andromeda Strain" written next to them as a tribute to Robert Wise.

"That's all we know, except that it's now 2.2. days from Earth."

— William Shatner as Capt. Kirk

Finally it is 1:00 PM, the pits are covered, the lights are set up, everything is ready. Robert Wise set up a special slide presentation to clue us in on what is going on. He projects special artist's concept slides on a blue Federation of Planets emblem that will later be the viewing screen. The screen will show the three Klingon ships being destroyed by some kind of cosmic cloud with relative ease. Kirk delivers a speech which is interrupted by a further transmission showing the destruction of one of our colonies on a minor planet, Epsilon 9. Many Enterprise crew members had family and friends on Epsilon 9. We make preparations for immediate departure. End of scene.

Filming is a long, slow, dull process. It means taking a short scene over and over again until it comes out correctly. Then the cameras are reset for a different angle and the same scene is shot again. Those bright interior lights are hot, and the whole process is slow and uncomfortable. The reason for all the frivolity reported on the *Star Trek* set was to combat the inevitable boredom that sets in. It is all part of the movie making process. The *Star Trek* fans were an extremely cooperative bunch. When director Wise said, "Places!" We were at our places and ready to witness again the terrible events and experience the emotional traumas that were part of the scene. Wise would talk us through the scene. "Now you see the enemy strike again. It's awesome. You're horrified! You can't believe it! React!" Finally the captain bids us to prepare and we grimly set about our duties. The fans put their all into it as if they really cared about what was transpiring.

Between takes we got drinks of water. Don, in his big head, claimed he was drowning in his own perspiration. James Doohan frequented the water cooler, sporting the mustache he had grown for *Jason of Star Command*.

I also talked with George Takei, receiving an okay to run a conversation with him that I had been part of and had transcribed. Nichelle Nichols and William Shatner were also there. This scene occurs before either McCoy or Spock are taken onboard, so DeForest Kelley and Leonard Nimoy were not present.

Shatner looked particularly good as he had trimmed down a bit for the role. At the start of the scene he strode out in his green and white admiral's uniform and he looked and acted every bit the James Kirk that we have come to know. Though it did not appear he would be on camera during any of that day's shooting, he went through his blocking with thorough professionalism and used his voice to convince everyone that they were indeed in the presence of James Kirk. Applause greeted him.

During the rest period, the ladies on the balcony rested their tired feet by sitting down and swinging their legs one way and then the other off the edge. David Gerrold walked up with a glint in his eye. "Does this mean we're on a Rockette-ship?" he asked. The ladies decided to spare him. Before much could be done, it was "places everyone" again.

Things were proceeding so well that it was decided to go into overtime. Since all the waivers were being paid full SEG scale, this meant a lot of extra money spent on the part of the studio. It also meant that the fans would not be coming back for a second day. This upset many fans because they had gone to great lengths to free themselves for the two days of shooting, and a few had traveled a long way. But less people were needed, and Guild minimums have to be met before any waivers can be kept on. Well, tiring and boring as it was, it had been a great day!

Also on the subject of payment, when Bjo first mentioned it to one fan, asking her if she would like to be in the movie, she added, "Oh, I forgot, there's money involved." "How much?" the fan asked. "$75.00 a day." "I guess I could manage that," replied the fan, be-

lieving that she would have to pay for the privilege of being in the film.

Towards the end of the shooting, I investigated the area underneath the blue Federation of Planets symbol. There was an alcove that contained pictures of various ships which had the name Enterprise. The first was a sailing ship, then the aircraft carrier, then the space shuttle, then a space wheel, and the familiar starship ended the panorama. It was quite a nice touch.

A photographer wandered in, and since no cameras were allowed on set, this was my only opportunity to have some photographic evidence outside of the film itself that I was ever in it. Three basic shots were taken; one for *Starlog* (see *Starlog* #20, page 32. I'm in the second row, far left, directly behind Bjo), one for *Future*, and one for Susan Sackett's *The Making of Star Trek: The Motion Picture* book. There also was a making of the film production short being made. I said goodbye to my uniform, for that would be the last I'd see of it until the film opened. While Paramount spent a lot of money on those uniforms, they were going to gather dust rather than being used as promotional outfits. But can you imagine the effect it would have if a fan walked into a convention wearing their Star Fleet uniform?

The threesome broke up to return to the dressing areas. (The threesome being Leigh, Don and I, who figured that some of the members aboard the Enterprise had to know one another, so we formed a cross-cultural triad. The only other group I knew about was Kathleen and Jay as the pair of redheads.) Marlene was up on the balcony, so she stayed behind for a final close-up shot.

The people on the balcony had been bored much of the time, and so while they were reacting seriously during the shots, they would watch the destruction of Epsilon 9 and say things like: "I'm glad they're dead. They deserved everything they got," and "All right, all right! Destroy the stupid planet!" Now that Robert Wise wanted them to emote the tears and tragedy of the scene, they had a hard time just keeping a straight face. Somehow, though, the scene got done to the director's demanding satisfaction.

"We didn't have any crisis that held us up, it's just in the nature of science fiction that things tend to take longer."

— Gene Roddenberry

It was time to go, so I left the soundstage through an exit which indicated the direction to the bowling alley and the archery range (sure, why not? After all, there must be some hard to use lengths of long, straight ship space), but instead of ending up at either of those two places, it was back to the dressing room. We waited for Marlene to finish up. It had been a long day. We decided to end it by taking Leigh out to have a pizza. Then Don, Marlene and I headed home for a case of complete exhaustion.

We could not tell how the *Star Trek* movie would turn out, but one thing had been demonstrated: there had been a lot of intelligence and planning behind this film. Pains had been taken to see that the ship seemed more liveable. The space was well utilized, even the large spaces for recreation (though with

the removal of the pits and the electronic shuffleboard, the recreation room resembled an auditorium, and why does the ship need one of those, particularly a two-storey one?). The costumes did look good, and each had a "belt buckle" which was supposed to be a biosystems readout gadget. (Aha! The return of the Feinberger!) I thought the designers had done a good job taking the *Star Trek* future into its future.

In any event, *Star Trek: The Motion Picture* ushered science fiction films into the 1980s. It was the return of the long-loved and long-cherished series that is enjoyed by so many across the world. Years from now I can just imagine pointing myself out as part of a science fiction film landmark. In any event I was proud just to be part of the magic.

*LASFS meets every Thursday night in Los Angeles at 11513 Burbank Blvd. Its membership includes many of the top fans and writers in the science fiction field.

**Bjo Trimble is the author of *The Star Trek Concordance*, and among other accomplishments started *Star Trek*'s first letter writing campaign (See *The World of Star Trek* by David Gerrold), and with her husband John chaired the excellent Equicon/Filmcon conventions.

This article is dedicated to all the people who made this experience possible, from Gene Roddenberry, who had the dream, to the fans who insisted that it did not have to end.

It seems like ancient history now, but once upon a time many people were upset that someone who wasn't real was going to die.

Spock's Death: Was It Worth The Uproar?

by James Van Hise

It was the summer of 1981. July, I should think, when the rumors first began to sift down from the top. Before long they had spread like wildfire. Everyone feared, "Paramount was up to its dirty tricks." And "They're going to kill Spock 'cause Nimoy wants too much money." Everyone feared Paramount wanted an object lesson for the other actors. A warning to stay in line or find their character dissolved forever in the finale, not unlike the Wicked Witch of the West.

What set this rumor aside from all the rest is that it had started at the top, with Gene Roddenberry. Susan Sackett spilled the Vulcan beans at a convention in Illinois, saying Gene Roddenberry opposed the idea. That it went against the optimistic grain which underlay all of *Star Trek*. The news spread so fast that the first fanzine I read about it in was a newsletter published in England. Still, the story hadn't hit the national media.

Then Roddenberry gave a talk somewhere and someone asked him about this rumor over the air (a plant?). He reluctantly admitted it was true. Shortly after this, the national press picked up the story. I can still recall watching the NBC news one night in November of '81 and seeing Jessica Savitch report that Mr. Spock was going to die in the next *Star Trek* movie. It took them four months longer to learn this than we did. (Woodward and Bernstein where were you? Why didn't you do a piece called *Spock: The Final Days* ?)

Then the now-famous ad appeared in *The Hollywood Reporter,* claiming a "survey" concluded that if Paramount *killed S*pock, it would result in $26 million less in box office receipts. Patrons would either refuse to watch or be too depressed to see it over and over. Repeat viewing provides the bread and butter, making up the one hundred million dollar box-office. Despite the huge box-office, not everyone in America has actually seen *E. T.* It just seems that way.

As fandom entered the home stretch, waiting to see *Star Trek II*, a new wrinkle entered the picture. The daily syndicated program *Entertainment Tonight* (produced by Paramount) reported the plans for Spock's death, along with a viewer phone-in poll. A vast majority voted nay, but a significant number

45

supported the idea. One friend of mine spent 50 cents for the phone call to vote in the affirmative just because he felt that someone should. Within two days, *Entertainment Tonight* reported that Leonard Nimoy had phoned them from China to assert that reports of his death were greatly exaggerated. How strange. A program produced by Paramount's television arm reports on a film being produced by its television arm and one of the principal actors denies the story? Was it all just a shabby publicity gimmick? That's what some would have you believe.

Starlog believed so, particularly after being given misleading information. This was later retracted, with blame for the erroneous details lay firmly at the feet of Paramount. An outraged Paramount thereafter gave *Starlog* the cold shoulder. Paramount finally relaxed this restriction but *Starlog*'s major pieces on *Star Trek II* only began appearing in May.

Then came the sneak preview in Kansas City. Fans interviewed coming out of the theater gave positive reports. Nimoy had coyly referred to the issue of his character's death by saying, "No one ever dies in science fiction." Would Spock pull a Ben Kenobi? Would he be lurking over Kirk's shoulder, festooned with a halo, whispering encouragement and/or sweet nothings?

Then came the film and we understood. Although Leonard Nimoy is doing his utmost to rewrite history and have us believe that his input was minimal, others close to the production state otherwise. It didn't come first-hand until Walter Koenig appeared at the San Diego Comic Convention in July of '82. He explained that Spock's death

did largely emerge from Leonard's wish to leave the role, but that after he began work on the film and had read the script, he changed his mind. This coincided with Nimoy landing major roles in Marco Polo and A Woman Called Golda. After that he no longer felt Spock was holding him back.

Nimoy would deny this now because he's well aware fans consider him a tool of the role, something which Roddenberry may have felt as well. Interestingly, Koenig noted Nimoy would be back in Star Trek III, an announcement not yet made by Paramount.

What did this whole donnybrook reveal? It revealed that some of us take our fantasy too seriously. Spock has no more independent reality than Superman or Spider-Man, yet fans were stricken over thoughts of his demise.

Yet it's just a movie, as David Gerrold ably pointed out, and that his death could be a good thing if it would teach us not to take all this so seriously. Enjoy it, but don't idolize it. Don't let celluloid death mean more than bitter realities. The death of one human being is of far more moment than a fictional demise. If one fictional character dies, we have others in each book we read or film we watch. A human being is unique and irreplaceable.

Some objected to the demise on different grounds. They didn't want to go to a movie to see a funeral and be exposed to powerful emotions. Yet a strong portrayal can make us appreciate life. Fantasy should enrich us. Our entertainment should challenge us.

This interview with William Shatner took place upon the release of Star Trek III: The Search For Spock and allowed the actor to look back on his years with Star Trek and speculate on the future of Captain Kirk.

Shatner Interview

by James Van Hise

Nearly every *Star Trek* adventure originates from Kirk's point of view and sweeps up the rest of the Enterprise crew. Needless to say, everyone depends on Captain Kirk, but not even he could snatch *Star Trek* from oblivion. That took an event which in itself was pretty cosmic—a film called *Star Wars*.

"I used to joke about driving by Paramount shortly after *Star Wars* opened," Shatner said, "and hearing a shot ring out because someone had committed suicide over losing that big opportunity. In typical fashion Paramount recovered from the shock and said, 'Well, if *Star Wars* made it, lets do a *Star Trek* in the same manner.'

"The series always had what I used to call the monster-of-the-week. That's the nature of episodic television. We liked to think that on the series there was a level of humanity and philosophy that stood out every so often. It was one of those elements that made the series ever so popular.

"When I first heard the conversations about *Star Trek I*, it was directly after the success of *Star Wars*. I think that the studio had always held back from doing anything with *Star Trek* because of their reluctance to believe that something like that could have a viable

economic life. Then *Star Wars* hit and became the major success it was."

Being such an intimate part of the phenomenon, Shatner is able to look back over the revivals and see the differences in texture which each has had.

"*Star Trek I* was, in my view, an attempt to catch up to *Star Wars* by spending 40 million dollars to match the special effects. Although it made a lot of money, it was not a terrific film. It was a good film, but it was not a terrific film. It was not in the real tradition of *Star Trek*. By that time everybody who really knew what the elements of *Star Trek* were had either moved away or gone on.

"Those of us who knew said, 'You need a close-up of the faces.' They said, 'A close-up? You're used to TV. This is movies! You need a grandiose style and epic proportions!' And so it began being their money, and they won. While it made them a great deal of money, it was not really *Star Trek*. They had a large box office return but they had spent so much money on it that they didn't have any profit. So they finally said, 'Lets spend less money and do what you guys want to do.' It's really by a confluence of economics that we came to do what we've done in these

47

last two shows.

"When we were doing the series, we didn't have much money for special effects," Shatner explained. "This forced us to do more human stories. Now we have more money but they want to save it for special effects so we're doing more human stories!"

The director shapes the style and vision of a film as much as does the script. Each director tends to contribute ideas to the screenplay. For instance, Nicholas Meyer contributed a great deal to the script of *Star Trek II: The Wrath of Khan*. For *The Search For Spock*, Leonard Nimoy requested that the villains be changed from Romulans to Klingons. Personalities and creativity tend to be inextricably linked in a motion picture production. If anyone works very closely with the director, it's the star.

"Each director had their own characteristics," Shatner recalled. "Robert Wise came to the first film with a justifiably legendary reputation. When he said you stand there and you go there, you said, 'Yes, sir.' He had won Oscars and this meant a great deal. He was indeed the father figure. Not that he didn't allow us certain freedoms, but he was Robert Wise, one of the great directors of Hollywood."

Concerning *Wrath of Khan*, Shatner stated, "Nick Meyer had written a script and we were in love with the script and impressed by his creative ability. So even though it was only the second picture he had directed, we felt that his imagination should be given full flower. And so here he was. He had written the script but hadn't directed very much. Whatever help we could give him was offered and he would accept it, or not accept it, depending on whether he thought we were correct. But he had written the script and had therefore brought to it another unquestionable aspect."

The Search For Spock was a unique situation in which one of the stars also served as the film's director.

"Leonard and I are the dearest of old friends," said Shatner. "We had shared a mutual struggle with the management in various stages, whether it was script, a thought, a concept or a dressing room. Whatever it was, we were always united. We'd go back to the dressing room and ask each other what we thought. We'd have a plan! Whenever we dealt with management we planned it out together.

"Now suddenly my 'brother' was saying, 'Well, you should do this and you should do that.' There was an awkward period of time for me, although I don't think for Leonard, where I felt alone in anything I might have objected to. From my point of view it was more awkward in the beginning than with either of the other two directors. But that slowly erased itself."

After one *Star Trek* star directed an entry of the series, the obvious question became whether William Shatner would follow suit. "That's a difficult question," he replied, "because I'm tied up at Columbia and I'm directing there on *T.J. Hooker*. But the truth of the matter is that I'd like to."

Despite the fact that *The Search For Spock* dovetails neatly with *The Wrath of Khan*, *Star Trek II* was not originally filmed with the sequel in mind. In fact, filming on *Star Trek II* completed before Nimoy changed his mind about wanting Spock's death to be permanent.

"It was never anticipated," Shatner revealed. "An accident happened. Maybe it wasn't an accident if you don't believe in accidents. It was really very strange.

"We were getting ready to do the death scene of Spock. This wasn't scripted, but Leonard put his hand on DeForest's head and he was looking for something mysterious to do. Spock was going to die because Leonard didn't want to play him anymore. He said he'd spent his adult life playing Spock and he wanted to go on to other things, because Spock was stifling his career and creative impulses. He needed to stop. It was very understandable, and while we were all grieved, we understood.

"But for some reason, in this last scene, Leonard said, 'Remember.' It was meaningful to someone in *Star Trek* but we didn't know what it meant. And that was the end. Spock was dead and the question was, will there be a *Star Trek III* and how could you do it without Spock? But that was a whole other question. As far as everyone was concerned at that time, Spock was dead.

"Then the possibility of Leonard directing the film came up. Leonard said, 'If I can direct the film, I'll play Spock.' But the problem was, how do you bring him back to life?"

A dilemma not easily solved! This is born out when examining the original story treatment written by Bennett for *Star Trek III* (then called "Return to Genesis"). Originally the mysterious "remember" didn't enter into the story although the Genesis planet did.

Shatner remembered that "Harve Bennett made a tremendous creative leap and used that 'Remember' to bring Spock back in a very valid science fiction way. Whether it was an accident or a chain of circumstances I just don't know."

Shatner felt he understood Leonard Nimoy's change of mind. "I would surmise that when Leonard was able to leverage his desire to direct against the very natural desire to grow and expand his horizons as an artist, that he wanted to direct the film. So he was able to use the leverage of them wanting him to do Spock with his desire to direct. Those who finally agreed made a deal that if he wanted to direct, he had to come back for the fourth *Star Trek*.

Fans have their own feelings regarding a Spock-less *Star Trek*, but what's Shatner's view? "I wouldn't even want to consider it," he stated flatly. "When asked what the ingredients are that make *Star Trek* so popular, you and I would point at the same things. They're the science fiction, the action, the philosophical undertone, the family of players and the cloak and the dagger. Whatever you point at, all those elements we know. But we still don't know why *Star Trek* is successful. There is a chemistry of a hit show there, but we don't know what it is. We just know that there are certain obvious parts. We don't really know the exact formula of *Star Trek* and therefore the danger of altering any of the elements is to alter the possibility that it might be successful or not.

"Obviously Leonard Nimoy as Mr. Spock is a major element, so he is essential."

What is *Star Trek*, really? What's it all about? What's its underlying message?

"That's like saying, 'What's the deep philosophical message of the Bible?' Although I must tell you that there were many segments where there was a desire to lay something in such as love and equality. At the same time, there was a *Star Trek* edict about letting aliens be themselves because of the diversity of life.

"Maybe if you want to sum up what *Star Trek* means as against 'Turn the other cheek' being the summation of Christianity, 'the diversity of life and its beauty' could be said to be what *Star Trek* is about."

During its original television run, one of the most important elements was *Star Trek*'s creator, Gene Roddenberry. Roddenberry is clearly the man who shaped what the series came to signify. Shatner's feeling about the presence of Roddenberry is somewhat different than his feeling about the presence of the Roddenberry-created characters, such as Spock.

"One day a father has to say to a child, 'Now you have to do it on your own. . . to grow beyond.' He is more like a technical adviser on the films now, rather than a creative force. Harve Bennett is the creative force behind these last two films. Harve looked at every one of the episodes to learn what *Star Trek* was. By immersing himself in it he has become as authoritative as anybody."

Star Trek II finally dealt with the obvious, that Captain Kirk is no longer the dashing 35-year-old starship captain he once was. They gave Kirk granny glasses, and yet this device was ignored in THE SEARCH FOR SPOCK. Or was it?

"It was there but they cut the scene out. It was in the scene when I was reviewing the tape to get a clue as to who was carrying Spock's marbles. It was a matter of the editing and I don't know why it wasn't kept.

"The objective thinking is that as each year goes by, as we all age, so does Captain Kirk. And I suppose there is a possibility that I'll wheel myself in sitting in a wheelchair and say, 'Press, um, that button there.' The idea is not to fight the aging process. Hopefully I will keep it at bay for a brief time to come. That's the objective view.

"The subjective one was of interest to me. This was because I was shooting *T.J. Hooker* last season and my contract with Paramount was made prior to my contract with Columbia, so that superseded the one with Paramount. *The Search For Spock* was supposed to happen during the hiatus. That's the period of time between the seasons of *Hooker*. Because of the exigencies involved with the movie business, it was delayed and kept on pushing back further than *T.J. Hooker* could take. There was a great deal of communication between the two studios. We decided to push up the season of *Hooker* as the movie got pushed back. When we stopped shooting on *Hooker,* we went immediately to shooting the *Star Trek* film. I stopped shooting on a Friday and the following Monday I was before the cameras on *The Search For Spock*. I continued to shoot the film. Then on the day after I finished *Star Trek,* I was back in front of the cameras on *T.J. Hooker.*

"Doing a series is really fatiguing. It's

up at five or six in the morning and that's how I went into the film, with that kind of exhaustion. I could even see that on my face as we started shooting the movie. We started shooting on the bridge and that's the first scene in the film. So that first shot of me is just coming off of *T.J. Hooker*. I looked haggard, fatigued, all of the things that happen on a series.

"As the ease of making a film began, I could see myself looking better. There was a brief time, of a week or so, that I had off just before the big fight scene with Kruge. I'd taken that week and gone to the beach. To me, my face looked totally different when I came back.."

Unlike Leonard Nimoy, William Shatner has never felt his Star Trek persona interfered with his career goals.

"The character of Captain Kirk is different because he is, in effect, the hero and heroes are universal. I never felt stifled in the series and I think that any actor would have paid the management money to receive half of the roles that I've been asked to do.

"I just love Captain Kirk and the way they've been writing him!"

Shatner does have some ideas as to where he would like to see Kirk go in the future, "I have two things that I'd like to see. They're contrasted and yet they're unified. I'd like to see romance again. And I would like to see gritty realism. You know, with hand-held cameras, dirt under the fingernails and real steel clanging doors.

"It seems to me that the best thing that we could do with STAR TREK is bring in some brilliant young director. I use

the word young in that he wouldn't be afraid to try new things or let stodgy tradition get in his way. It may be someone who has never dealt with science fiction or indeed someone who has handled science fiction, but not Star Trek."

Captain James Tiberius Kirk, the commanding role on STAR TREK.

This is the only complete report on the ceremony when Gene Roddenberry received his star on the Hollywood Walk of Fame. Enterprise Incidents covered it from the front row!

Gene Roddenberry On The Hollywood Walk Of Fame

by James Van Hise

The stars came out early on September 4, 1985, to honor the man who created *Star Trek*. Nearly all the stars from the series attended, including Leonard Nimoy, Deforest Kelley, James Doohan, Walter Koenig, Nichelle Nichols, George Takei and Majel Barret. Also on hand were Roger C. Carmel, Susan Oliver, Fred Phillips and Grace Lee Whitney—and if you have to ask who any of those folks are, go back and re-read your *Star Trek Compendium*. William Shatner was unable to attend due to work commitments.

The unveiling of this star was the culmination of over a year of lobbying efforts by fans, spearheaded by Susan Sackett. Donations paid the $3,000.00 fee for the star and the ceremony. It was touch and go for a while because many names are nominated each year but only a select few are chosen. Roddenberry is the first writer to be so honored. This caused a minor furor among Hollywood insiders, but more on that later.

The ceremony began at 12:30 p.m. on an overcast day. As the Los Angeles Police Pipe Band broke into a rousing bagpipe melody prior to the festivities, the clouds parted.

Jimmy Doohan's loud voice bellowed in the background, "I hear people saying, 'I heard that David Gerrold says that Jimmy Doohan is dead.' Why don't you call me up?" he asked the writer. The guests laughed at the good humor that Doohan displayed after his recent ailments.

As Usual, Johnny Grant, the "Honorary Mayor of Hollywood" and chairman of the Walk of Fame committee, served as Master of Ceremonies.

With a recording of "Hooray for Hollywood" playing over the loud speakers, the festivities began.

Grant kicked everything off by saying, "Hello, everybody, and welcome to another Walk of Fame ceremony. Today we honor the creator and producer of the original *Star Trek* television series, Gene Roddenberry!" Cheers greeted the mention of the honored guest's

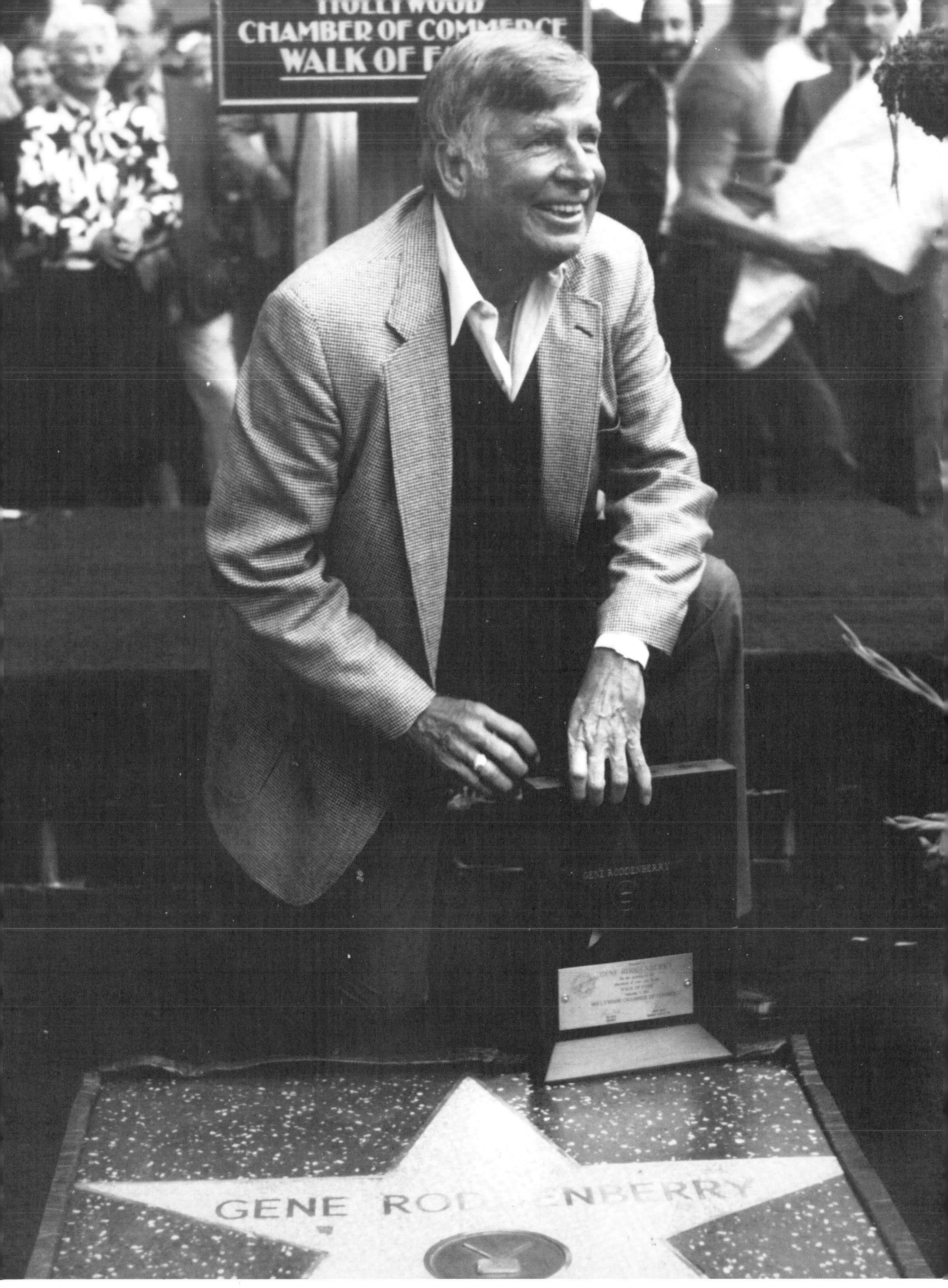
GENE RODDENBERRY

name.

Grant continued, "I also want to say that we welcome to Hollywood Trekkies from all over the world! Not just the United States; I know there is one who came all the way from Japan, and another from Switzerland; but we welcome all of you to this very special ceremony today."

Grant introduced Bill Welsh, President of the Hollywood Chamber of Commerce (the sponsoring organization of the Walk of Fame). Welsh stated, "I am particularly thrilled that today we honor a man who has had a long association with our community of Hollywood. Indicative of the fact that the whole world loves him are the people who have come from so many far away places to be a part of this ceremony today. Johnny's going to tell you more

about Gene Roddenberry and the things he has done here in Hollywood, as well as what you know about the *Star Trek* activities. This is our chance as a part of the Hollywood community to say to Gene, 'We want the world to know that we love you and that we respect you!' and Gene, we have a slogan in the Hollywood Chamber of Commerce — we says that we're building the Hollywood for the 21st century. That means, Gene, that when the next century rolls around and people walk up and down Hollywood Boulevard as you used to, they'll see this star and they'll know that this community had this great affection for you, and was proud that you were one of us who went on to great heights of success."

Grant then read some telegrams received from friends and supporters who had not been able to attend the ceremony, who still wanted to convey their feelings publicly.

"Congratulations Big Bird - to the creator and prime spirit, it will be a pleasure to walk on you. The Vulcans send their love -Mark Leonard."

Then he read, 'Dear Gene, everywhere I go, I hear your name on the lips of people saying how incredible is the talent of Roddenberry for having written the *Martian Chronicles*. At the same time, everywhere you go, do you not hear the magic name Ray Bradbury, who created *Star Trek*? No matter how you play it, isn't it wonderful? Love to you on this special, fine day -Ray Bradbury!"

Grant then introduced Gene by giving a brief rundown of his accomplishments.

"Gene Roddenberry has led a life as exciting as nearly any high adventure fiction. A native Texan who spent his youth in Los Angeles, he later studied aeronautical engineering at UCLA. During World War II he served as a pilot and flew 89 sorties. He was decorated with the Distinguished Flying Cross and the Air Medal. It was during this time that he began to write, selling stories to flying magazines and later poetry to such publications as the *New York Times*. After the war, he continued to fly for Pan American World Airways - until he saw television for the first time. Correctly estimating television's future, he left his flying career behind and moved to Hollywood. While establishing himself as a writer, he joined the Los Angeles Police Department. Soon, he was selling scripts to such shows as *Good Year Theatre, Dragnet, Naked City* and many others. Es-

Gene Roddenberry receives his star on the Hollywood Walk of Fame as the cast and crew who made it possible watch. Fans from throughout the world raised the money to pay for the star and ceremony. Roddenberry was the first writer to be so honored.

tablished as a writer, he turned in his badge and become a free-lancer. Later he was head writer for the highly popular television series, *Have Gun, Will Travel*. *Star Trek* followed in 1966, and we all know the rest is history.

"*Star Trek* later went on to win science fiction's coveted Hugo Award and was the first television series to have an episode preserved in the Smithsonian Institute. In 1979, Roddenberry produced *Star Trek: The Motion Picture,* which led to the sequels *Star Trek II: The Wrath of Khan* and *Star Trek III: The Search For Spock.* He is the executive consultant for all *Star Trek* films. Gene is in steady demand as a lecturer and a keynote speaker for such organizations as NASA, the Smithsonian institute, the Library of congress and top universities. He has served as a member of the Writer's Guild Executive Council, is a former governor of the Television Academy of Arts and Sciences, and is a member of the board of the directors of the National Space Institute. The father of three, Gene lives in Los Angeles with his lovely wife Majel.

"Ladies and Gentlemen, family, friends, and Trekkies from around the world, please help me and the Hollywood Chamber of Commerce give a warm welcome to Mr. Gene Roddenberry as we dedicate to him this star on the Hollywood Walk of Fame. Scottie, beam him aboard!"

Bill Welsh gave Gene a special Walk of Fame jacket emblazoned with Gene's name. One Maria Hernendez from City Councilman Michael Woo's office then stated, "The Mayor has proclaimed today Gene Roddenberry Day and the council has said, ' Now therefore be it resolved that the City Council of the

city of Los Angeles congratulates Mr. Roddenberry on his many accomplishments and wishes him continued success.'"

Then some guests were introduced to the assembled multitude.

Leonard Nimoy stated, " This is a wonderful day for Gene, obviously, and for all of us connected with *Star Trek*. I'll tell you just one brief story. When we were preparing the series, I wasn't sure that the ears were going to work out right, and I thought if these ears don't work, I'm going to be Dumbo of the year. So I went to Gene and said, 'I'm really nervous about it Gene.' Before we started shooting I said maybe we should just drop the ears because they don't look right, and he said, 'I'll tell you what. You wear them for thirteen weeks and if it doesn't work out, we'll get you an ear job.'

"Gene, I'm glad you talked me into it. Congratulations today. I think it's wonderful for you, wonderful for *Star Trek*, and we're really happy to be here with you to celebrate."

When Walter Koenig spoke, he stated, "Not only is Mr. Roddenberry an extraordinary man and a gentleman we all admire, but he is also the very first writer to be honored on the Hollywood Walk of Fame."

Johnny Grant quickly jumped in to add, "Just to keep the record straight, he has several colleagues who are already here. There has been much controversy over this. He is being honored today for everything he did in television."

A mini-controversy had indeed grown over Roddenberry's receiving the star, because he was the first writer who wasn't also an actor or director to be granted one. This tended to make the Writer's Guild look bad since they had nothing to do with nominating him nor had they nominated any other writers in their membership for the honor. The fact that Roddenberry is also a producer helped blur whether he was being honored solely as a writer.

On with the speeches.

Nichelle Nichols: "Gene Roddenberry, I'm so proud of you, as I've always been. I'm so grateful to you for thinking of Uhura, and my hailing frequencies are always open for you!"

Harve Bennett, the producer of *Star Trek II through V*, noted: "I have only one word for a man who makes what has followed his genius so easy, and that is Mazel tov!"

When Roddenberry finally spoke after all the glowing praise from his friends and colleagues, he voiced his thoughts about this special moment in his life.

"As a Los Angeles policeman, I walked on this boulevard on foot patrol, and to have a star here is a double pleasure. Actually, when I walked the boulevard as a Los Angeles policeman, my scripts were beginning to sell and my producers didn't know I was a policeman. I was afraid if they found out they might not buy them. I spent my time here on Hollywood Boulevard jumping from one dark doorway to another.

"It's doubly great to have the Scots section of the Los Angeles police band here."

Gene then introduced his mother and his son, Gene Jr., his two daughters and his brother Bob. He then introduced his sister, whom he described as, "a much

better writer than I am."

Clearly nervous, surrounded as he was by people who were there to pay him tribute, Roddenberry stated, "I want to thank some other people, too. When I go places, people often ask me, what are Trekkies? What are *Star Trek* fans? Some of them got an idea that they are people who dress in funny clothes and go around making signs and so on. Some of them do that and have fun doing that, but *Star Trek*'s Trekkies range the entire audience and include astronauts, physicians, physicists and yes, they also include twelve and fourteen year old kids. We have also been associated with *Star Trek* for almost twenty years now, and in twenty years I have never had a bad experience with a *Star Trek* fan. They're incredible people and I want you to applaud them! They are people who believe in humanity and believe they are going to make it.

"I also concur with you folks on this Hollywood Boulevard. This city, Los Angeles, is the twenty-first century city in the making. It is becoming a Third World city; I think that's marvelous. The mixture of races and colors and religions here says that democracy, dement, does work and it's a great thing and you haven't seen anything yet. The Los Angeles that's ahead of us, if we can keep peace and order on our streets, we can become anything we want and do anything we want to do in Los Angeles. And I think we will."

When asked to do the introduction from the *Trek* TV series, Roddenberry drew a blank, and even with coaxing wasn't able to recall it at all. Finally, he laughed and said, 'I just write these things. I'm not a performer. I believe them all and I believe in humanity, and

I'm not done writing about humanity. We are an incredible species. You've seen Los Angeles, you've just seen humanity. We're still just a child-creature. We're still being nasty to each other around the world and all the children go through those phases, but we are growing up and moving into adolescence, now. When we grow up, man, we are going to be something and we're going to do it, too!

"Thank you all so very much. Thank all of you that came out and bless you all."

When Roddenberry finally saw the star unveiled, his friends surrounded him. Johnny Grant said, "Ladies and gentlemen, we welcome to the Walk of Fame, Gene Roddenberry!" And the crowd cheered and applauded.

The moment had arrived. *Star Trek* had really made a star out of its creator. The 1,810th on the Hollywood Walk of Fame, located at 6683 Hollywood Boulevard, serves as a lasting tribute to the imagination behind the spirit that endures — the spirit of *Star Trek*.

Whenever STAR TREK adds something new to the world of entertainment, it's an event.

The Universal Experience

by James Van Hise

On June 9, 1988, Universal Studios launched its own addition to *Star Trek*. A gigantic balloon in the shape of the Enterprise hovered over the top floor of the huge parking garage proclaiming the event. While the balloon was by no means full scale, it was about forty weeks long and well crafted so that there was no mistaking it for anything except The Enterprise.

The unveiling of this latest addition to the Universal Studios Tour was set for 10 AM with the Press and a few hundred selected fans in attendance. As with most anything like this, it ran late, not starting until about 10:30. The bridge set was crowded with people. Camera crews tried to keep out of each other's way while Gene Roddenberry stood to one side being interviewed. Deforest Kelley was answering questions when William Shatner arrived and walked up to his costar, giving Kelley a good-natured hug. Also on hand were George Takei, Nichelle Nichols, James Doohan and Walter Koenig, although the fans in the audience would not know who was there for the show until later.

In front of the stage, the fans became restless. They began chanting, "Star Trek, Star Trek, Star Trek." Then, finally, there was Star Trek!

The Star Trek Event at Universal Studios in Studio City (just north of Hollywood) is housed in a large auditorium capable of seating hundreds of people. Above the stage hang three large screens showing projected images viewed easily from anywhere in the auditorium. A film narrated by William Shatner which told the history of *Star Trek* began to unreel. It showed choice scenes and selected dialogue from the original series, then moved on to clips from each of the movies, finally climaxing with sequences from *Star Trek*: The Next Generation. Unfortunately, the audio portion proved inaudible for the first half of the couple minute mini-history.

Captain Kirk asks his computer to display the history of the Enterprise, beginning with its first Captain, Christopher Pike. It goes on to display mini-profiles of each crew member, beginning with Spock, showing snippets from "This Side of Paradise" and "Amok Time." Leonard McCoy comes next in such lines of dialogue as, "I'm a doctor, not a brick-layer!" "I'm a doctor, not an engineer!" and "I'm a doctor not an escalator!" Finally the film offers several versions of the immortal "He's dead, Jim." Brief descriptions of the movies follow, with reference to the new Enterprise. Kirk then asks the

59

computer to extrapolate into the future to see what the next generation might be like. This leads into descriptions of Jean-Luc Picard and company. The film ends with Captain Kirk saying, "Happy birthday, Enterprise. Let's see what's out there." Then, one after the other, all three versions of the Enterprise enter warp speed.

Following the film, a generic host dressed in a dark suit stepped out from behind the curtain. He announced: "Universal Studios Tour welcomes you to the premiere of Paramount Pictures *Star Trek* Adventure. And a special welcome to the fifteen hundred fans who, as contest winners, are here to celebrate this premiere with us. Just prior to you coming into the theatre this morning, we went out and selected twenty-nine members from your group and they're going to participate as stars in our very first episode. My name is Jerry Green and I'm going to be director for our show today and I have to be real honest with you here, I'm a little nervous. Usually before openings of shows you get nervous butterflies, but when you're doing a show based on *Star Trek* for fifteen hundred people who know almost everything there is to know about *Star Trek*, you want somebody here who is..."

Whereupon Gene Roddenberry steps out from behind the curtain and receives thunderous acclaim from the audience. "Ladies and Gentlemen," Green continues, "the creator of *Star Trek*, Mr. Gene Roddenberry!"

"Thank you so much," states Gene, beaming proudly. "You're very kind. I love you all; I really do."

"Mr. Roddenberry," Green states, "I'm glad you showed up, believe me. I can see me making a mistake on some of this *Star Trek* knowledge and these guys would nail me to the cross!"

"Well why not, they do me!" quips Gene.

"They wouldn't dare. Listen, as long as you're here and because you know more than anybody; you've worked with cast, you've worked with crew. You've been around the fans for many, many years, what can you tell me that might help me get through this alive?"

"Well," Gene adds, "I think that the important thing is for us not to depend on our own cleverness so much, but depend on what is basically with the fans. They are the ones who make *Star Trek* possible because they believe in the things we talked about, and the Networks and others have never really believed the fans were of the quality group that they are, but they are wonderful and they make all this possible."

Green then announced that they were going to proceed with the event and we were all going to watch as they made a movie.

A recorded vo*ice welcom*ed the audience to this behind-the-scenes experience in motion picture and television production. "You are about to go where you have never gone before, as Universal Studios and Paramount Pictures proudly present: The *Star Trek* Adventure!"

The curtain on stage has opened to reveal a duplicate of the bridge of the Enterprise as seen in the motion pictures. A number of the fans selected while waiting in line appear dressed in the red uniforms seen in *Star Trek* II, III and

All aboard for the STAR TREK EXPERIENCE at Universal Studios. Pictured left to right standing are Walter Koenig, Deforest Kelley, Nichelle Nichols, Gene Roddenberry and James Doohan. George Takei is shown seated.

IV. They sit at consoles and control panels.

"Ladies and gentlemen," Green continues, "we are going to shoot footage exactly the way it's done for the movies. When we're finished, through our amazing instant edit system, we're going to put it all together so that we can watch the results together. You are looking at the bridge, obviously, of the

most of the time easy. Easy like opening a door! Give it your best shot there, Jeff. Let's see how you do."

One of the fans sitting on stage apparently pulls a lever and a turbo-lift door opens—and out steps William Shatner! The fans explode into applause since not everyone knew he was back stage.

"Ladies and gentlemen, Captain Kirk himself, William Shatner!" The cheer,

starship Enterprise and we have here seasoned veterans. They've endured years, er, *minutes* of rigorous training so that they can put up with all this. It takes more than actors to make a movie. It takes stage crew. A few minutes ago, when we selected people from the audience, we cast Jeff. He's going to work as a stage hand in our show. Sometimes his job might be difficult,

applauding and shouting continues. "You guys have to stop meeting like this," Green states.

"Just as Gene predicted, twenty years ago!" quips Shatner about what's happening around them. The audience laughs.

"Mr. Shatner, I lied a few moments ago. These guys are not seasoned veterans," Green admits. "This is their first time, so you being the Captain here, maybe you could offer them some words of advice on how to complete this?"

"Get off the ship!" Shatner shouts. "That's all I can come up with at the moment," the actor admits.

"I'm sure they'll take that to heart," Green replies. "Ladies and gentlemen, Mr. Shatner will be back again in just a short while. Right now, how about a big round of applause—Mr. William Shatner!"

As Shatner waves and returns backstage, no one in the audience realizes that he doesn't plan to hang around. He will be long gone when everyone assembles on stage nearly an hour later after the main program.

"He's going to engineering to take care of some stuff there with Scotty," Green says as Shatner completes his exit. "Now let's relax. We are all set to do this. Now keep in mind that in our storyline, the Enterprise and their arch enemies the Klingons have been summoned to this planet for some mysterious reason. They don't know why, and when they get there they find that there's a blue energy force that is causing strange phenomenon to happen on the planet. All right. Don, are you ready to shoot our first scene?"

"We've already got it, Jerry," a voice states from a loudspeaker overhead.

"I guess we must be dragging our feet; you guys are fast!" the director replies. "Your crew work that fast?" he asks Gene.

"Never," answers Roddenberry.

"Usually they wait for the director, but not this time. We'll go ahead with our next scene. Enterprise crew, when I say action, I want you all to look at this corner of the set and imagine something terrible." Dramatic background music from the TV series begins to play over the sound system. "Here we go, rolling cameras, and action! Everybody turn, look up at the corner of the set, mouth wide open!" A young lady on stage tries to act but keeps smiling from embarrassment at being in front of such a huge audience.

Then Jerry says cut. "Good job. See how easy it is? When you have the right talent on stage it's easy to make a movie. Let's try it again. This time we're going to go to that corner of the set, okay? You got it?"

"Pretend it's a network executive and he's telling you you're being cancelled," Roddenberry adds. The audience groans and laughs.

"Them or our show," Jerry asks. "That's good. We'll go with that. That's better than the line I had!" Once again the music rolls and the "actors" act while dramatic music accompanies the "action." When that's completed, he has three of the fans on stage do their individual dialogue, which is recorded into a microphone where they're seated and is inaudible to the audience, which is asked to remain silent during these moments. We'll hear the dialogue when it's inserted into the "movie" shown as the climax of the program.

Green walks up to a young man seated at the navigation console. "Do you know what chair you're sitting in?"

"Sorry?" he replies, not understanding at first what Jerry asked him.

"You don't have to be sorry. What chair

Fans dressed in Starfleet and Klingon costumes appear with Roddenberry and the STAR TREK crew for the making of a very special film as part of the premiere of the STAR TREK EXPERIENCE at Universal Studios.

are you sitting in? Mr. Chekov usually sits here, you know that? Do you know Mr. Chekov is Russian? Are you Russian?"

"No."

"Good, because we don't want you a rushin' in on your line." The audience groans in despair over the bad pun and boos.

"They turn so fast, don't they?" Green

you tell them," he asks Gene.

"Well we've never had that happen, so it's a new idea," Roddenberry deadpans.

They shoot a scene in which the people are supposedly being thrown back and forth on the stage. Then they step back and a different set rolls out on stage—the engineering set.

"Now we all know that the Enterprise

asks, rhetorically. "Writers are on strike, obviously. I guess they didn't go out soon enough." Green then has his "actors" perform another scene for the camera, this time jumping up and down and applauding. For another scene he explains that the Enterprise is being shaken and squeezed by some unknown force.

"We need them to react, so what would

doesn't go anywhere without Scotty and his engineering team, and when the going gets tough it's obviously Scotty and his guys that keep those warp engines going."

Nichelle Nichols and James Doohan come out, followed by a group of fans dressed in the white radiation suits seen on members of the engineering team in the movies.

"Commander Uhura, what are you doing down here in engineering? This isn't your usual turf?"

"Oh, I left someone to cover for me at Communications, but I had to come down here because every time I go to do a hailing frequency, I get this crazy bagpipes with Scottish music. I want to know why, Mr. Scott?" Nichelle asks, turning to Jimmy Doohan.

In his good-natured Scottish brogue, he replies, "Well you do have to know that I don't play the pipes but I finger them beautifully. And also, I would just like to say, *Captain, Uhura just can't take it!*"

"I'm afraid!" Nichelle replies, laughing.

"Scotty, what might you tell our engineering crew, they're novices at this, about keeping this thing going at warp speed," Jerry asks.

"Well, I tell ya' what, they gotta' shovel an awful lot a' coal, I mean crystals. Okay? As long as they keep on doin' that, you know, we got it made!"

"Ladies and gentlemen, how about a nice round of applause for Nichelle Nichols and James Doohan! We'll see them a little bit later. Mr. Roddenberry, in this particular scene the Enterprise obviously is under attack. Some things have gone wrong. The matter/anti-matter drive has broken a fan belt so these guys have to get everything fixed. Say that three times fast, all right?"

Jerry runs the fans through their scenes, which consists of having them look busy at work as well as having them dealing with smoke drifting over the scene. One made up with smudge marks looks as though he just staggered out of an explosion of some kind.

Then the next set rolls out and Jerry announces, "Ladies and gentlemen, we are proud to announce, an actual working transporter room. You've heard Captain Kirk say it a million times, *Beam me up, Scotty!* Ladies and gentlemen, through special authorization and permission by Mr. Roddenberry, this is a working transporter room. Let's step over here, Mr. Roddenberry."

"Amazing. I've never seen this before," says Roddenberry in mock amazement.

"Gee, I don't believe him. I don't know why," Jerry replies. He instructs the fans to get into position on the set. "Be very still. Last time we did this in rehearsal, somebody moved and they wound up with their hand stuck in their ear. So be real careful. Be still, and stand by and energize to those predetermined coordinates." The transporter effect, seemingly created live on the stage, looks very real. It elicits many oohs and ahs from the audience, although they don't reveal what the gimmick is they use to achieve the effect.

"I've never seen this before, really," Roddenberry insists, and he seems genuinely impressed.

"Ladies and gentlemen, I hope those four aren't related to any of you because they are gone. We weren't kidding around about that. Don, do you remember what the predetermined coordinates were? I forgot. Great, the Romulan nebula! Holy moley, have you ever had this happen in your show? I told you guys to be still, didn't I? You moved!"

Gerry walks over to a group of fans

made up like aliens with oversized heads. "I hope you know you look ridiculous. Due to a peace treaty with the Klingon empire, we have some members of the cultural exchange commission here to do our next scene with us, so ladies and gentlemen, without further delay, here are those ever loving Klingons!"

As the Klingon bridge set swings out on stage, so does DeForest Kelley, seated in the captain's chair next to a green Klingon dog. The dog is also one of the chosen fans in a costume.

"What do you think of our Klingon dragon-hound," Jerry asks him.

"I'm a doctor, not an animal trainer!" he shouts as the fans applause, "But in this case I'll make an exception."

"That's terrific. We sure appreciate you coming on and sharing this moment with us."

"It's a pleasure to be here and it's a pleasure to be on a Klingon ship," Kelley replies. "I've always felt when I was on one of these things that I needed something to cling on to." Kelley waves and returns back stage while Jerry Green starts organizing his Klingons. He walks over to the fans dressed as Klingons seated on the Klingon bridge set. One is in the captain's chair while three are at a console. Their elaborate costumes include head pieces with the ridge of bone across their head. The effect is spoiled somewhat because one of the Klingons wears glasses.

"These guys are brave, proud and ob*viously d*ownright nasty," Jerry observes. "Trained to kill instantly w*ith their* bare hands. This, of course, is the Cap-

tain's personal pet; this is a Klingon dragon-hound. You know I know a dog-groomer in Beverly Hills; maybe a poodle cut, a couple bows here and there." The dragon-hound looks up at him. "I guess not. Captain, keep an eye on your pet. The last time we were doing this he got loose in the audience. A terrible mess. Terrible mess. All right, gang. Listen carefully now. You're on our turf so if you do well we'll pick up your contract, and if you don't you can get a gig maybe as a heavy metal band. Stay with us. A few basic stage directions. First off, there is no taking of hostages. Do not fire disruptors indoors, okay? No looting. If you chew off an arm you must give it back."

The director then gives them stage directions so that the Klingons react to something at stage right and the Captain pets his dragon-hound. He then has the Klingons read their dialogue, which is loud and in Klingonese. When one of them is giving his line to the Klingon captain, the captain ad-libs a response, in Klingonese, of course. During another scene, the captain ad-libs another line. "Where is the captain getting these lines from?" Jerry wonders aloud. "Well if he's dying to say a line, we'll let him say a line. Your last line, captain. When I point to you, really give it to us. Now it's important that when you say this line, that you really punch the last word. Put your teeth together and seethe as you say it." Jerry turns to the audience and remarks, "This time he'll forget his line!"

After the Klingon portion of the preliminary performance concludes, Jerry congratulates them. Then they all stand up and take a bow. He has them exit the stage, remarking, "By the way, don't call us, we'll call you. They're probably running to their agent's office right now. I heard the captain had a face-lift not too long ago; I don't think it took. But speaking of face-lifts, ladies and gentlemen, how about a big round of applause also for our Klingon dragon-hound!" The hound removes its head mask, revealing a teenage boy underneath while the audience loudly applauds.

While they are preparing to roll off the Klingon bridge set, George Takei and Walter Koenig walk out on stage, the last of the special guests appearing there that day. Again the audience breaks into cheers and applause while George gives them the Vulcan salute.

"Gentlemen, we're very glad you could come out and be with us," says Jerry in welcoming them aboard. "You fellas have helped the Enterprise through lots and lots of problems. What do you think you might tell us about getting our landing party back that we beamed down?"

"Well, it's a life, but not as we know it," Takei replies, in a non-sequiter obviously written for him and which just somehow doesn't fit in as an answer to the question.

"That was so eloquently put that I have nothing to add to it," says Walter, feeling the attention turned to him. He gives a salute in Russian to "Lou and Sid and all the gang" in the black tower at Universal.

The pair then leave the stage amid more applause.

"Now ladies and gentlemen, in Hollywood, you can go from one side of the galaxy to the other simply by walking from one sound stage to another. Maybe make a change in sets and add some lighting or props or whatever. When we put this set together, you'll see how different it looks when things start falling into place."

Falling? That's what the audience wonders about. The alien set consists of a group of surface details and a backdrop lowered from the ceiling. It is an approach not that different from a number of the TV episodes.

"If you're wondering what happened to our landing party, this is where they ended up. Right here. Can we get our Enterprise group?" The landing party walks out, and are told to stand in position very still. They are now being photographed beaming down on the planet's surface. Then they have one of them step out and read a line of dialogue as though he's reporting in to Captain Kirk.

Green then turns to Gene again. "Mr. Roddenberry, are you a native Californian?"

"No, Texan."

"How long have you been here?"

"About 55 years," Roddenberry replies.

"Then you are well experienced in our next thing. We're going to have an eight point O earthquake on this set." He turns to the fans in uniform. "So when I say action, gang, we want you rockin' and rolling. Imagine you're slam dancing on a waterbed. However, don't leave the set. Stay on the set when you're doing all this, all right?"

The "earthquake" scene comes off well. Then the Klingons come out to film a scene in which the humans and Klingons throw rocks at each other. These

A fan dressed as a Klingon dog steals the show from Deforest Kelley and Gene Roddenberry.

aren't just little rocks but boulders obviously made out of some material to weigh about as much as a dry sponge. Then the "special effects" come out, which consist of long tentacles hanging from a track in the ceiling. The Klingons become captives of the tentacles until the Enterprise crewmen free them.

"I think we've uncovered a lot of talent here today," Roddenberry remarks.

looking the audience we see a scene in space. Then the Enterprise emerges from a dazzling display of special effects (the scene close to the end of *Star Trek*: The Motion Picture when the Enterprise emerges from V'ger over Earth). The powerful Jerry Goldsmith score plays.

William Shatner's voice says, "Captain's Log Stardate 4121.7. We are in

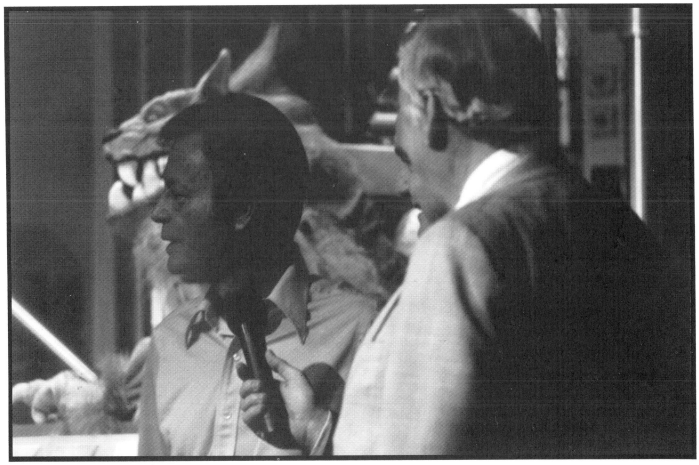

"Well, we'll cover it back up. Don't worry," Green quips. "We are now going to watch all of this put together in one composite package. We we like to thank Paramount Pictures for making this all possible, and now ladies and gentlemen, Universal Studios, Paramount Pictures and our guest actors, and Mr. Roddenberry, proudly present—The *Star Trek* Adventure!"

The lights dim and on the screens over-

route to Akimov VII, an obscure planet in the Klingon Neutral Zone. Our mission is to answer the distress call of a marooned space freighter which is carrying an invaluable cargo. I am confidant in the capabilities of my new crew who are seasoned professionals, the best assembled crew in the entire Starfleet Command. I am proud to serve with them."

The final production Intercuts scenes from *Star Trek* II with video of the fans in costume. It *makes for* jarring transitions since film and video look so different. You certainly can distinguish the new scenes from the real sequences from *Star Trek*.

The voice-over (which, of course, is all brand new) continues. "So far, all attempts to contact the crippled ship have been unsuccessful."

We see a scene with Uhura where she says, "This is Enterprise call. . . it's no use."

"All sensors read negative, sir," a fan recites in a video insert.

"There are two possibilities," says Spock, in a snippet from THE WRATH OF KHAN "They are unable to respond. They are unwilling to respond."

A strange blue light attacks the Enterprise. Then we see the Klingon bird of prey from THE SEARCH FOR SPOCK with the same blue glow surrounding it. The Klingons think that this is a new weapon of the Federation and they fire on the Enterprise. In classic shots from THE WRATH OF KHAN, the Enterprise sustains hits. The fans in Engineering toss about while smoke fills the room. This scene intercuts with one of Scotty from THE WRATH OF KHAN reporting the damage.

"Damage report," Kirk asks.

Spock is seen looking at the schematic of the Enterprise, pointing at the damage points as he turns to Kirk and says, "They knew exactly where to hit us."

"Uhura, patch me in," Kirk commands.

"Aye, sire," she replies, all in scenes from WRATH OF KHAN. Shatner's new voice-over follows.

"This is Captain James T. Kirk aboard the starship Enterprise. Our mission here is a peaceful one. We mean you no harm."

The Klingons are about to attack again when one proclaims, in subtitled translation: WE'VE LOST ALL POWER, SIR! His dialogue appears in Klingonese.

"Captain's Log, supplemental. We are locked in a helpless stand off with a Klingon bird of prey which is either unwilling or unable to finish us off. We have only life support and transporter systems remaining in operation. Our only option is to beam down to Akimov VII where we hope to retrieve dilithium crystals to properly channel power to our warp engines."

The video segment shows the landing party beaming down and one of them reports, "There is no sign of life anywhere!" Then there's seemingly a quake on the planet. "Something strange is happening here, sir!" he proclaims into his communicator. "Our tricorder's gone crazy!"

"Spock?" asks Kirk, on the bridge.

"Scanning," Spock replies.

The Klingons have beamed down and the commander states: DESTROY THEM! An energy bolt hits the Klingon weapon, neutralizing it. Since their weapons don't work, the Klingons and the Enterprise landing party hurl huge rocks at each other. Suddenly huge tentacles come into view and attack the Klingons, trapping them helplessly. We hear the roar of the weird monstrosity, which looks like some type of giant

It's the final salute at the premiere of the STAR TREK EXPERIENCE at Universal Studios.

space octopus. The Federation personnel rush in and save the Klingons, untangling them from the tentacles. The giant space octopus flies away and seems to disappear into space.

"You have robbed me of my honor!" the Klingon captain declares. "I demand that you kill me immediately!"

"Just go," says one of the Federation landing party, "and leave us in peace."

BEAM US UP IMMEDIATELY the subtitle states, and the Klingons beam up to their ship. Did I mention that one of the Klingons is wearing glasses?

In space, the space octopus appears and attacks the Enterprise, its tentacles wrapping around the hull and squeezing it so that the people inside rock back and forth. Didn't I see this on VOYAGE TO THE BOTTOM OF THE SEA

The grand opening of the Universal Studios STAR TREK AD-VENTURE in 1988 concluded with an epilogue starring Leonard Nimoy!

Leonard Nimoy and the Star Trek Adventure

by James Van Hise

When the Universal Studios "*Star Trek* Adventure" opened June 9, 1988, most of the original cast from *Star Trek* appeared for the grand premiere. Although Leonard Nimoy had been unavailable that morning, he later made a special afternoon appearance at the Universal Studios attraction on October 1, 1988. Ads promoting the appearance ran in Los Angeles newspapers and the following press release was issued:

LEONARD NIMOY ("MR. SPOCK") TO VISIT UNIVERSAL STUDIOS TOUR'S "STAR TREK ADVENTURE," SAT, OCT. 1

Leonard Nimoy, known to millions of *Star Trek* fans as "Mr. Spock" from the original television series and top-grossing motion pictures, will make a special appearance at Universal Studios Tour on Saturday, Oct. 1. Nimoy will be visiting Paramount's "*Star Trek* Adventure," the Tour's latest attraction, where he will participate in informal Q&A's with Tour visitors at 1:30 p.m. and 4:00 p.m.

Nimoy not only starred in the original *Star Trek* television series created by Gene Roddenberry as well as the four Paramount motion pictures, he also directed "*Star Trek*s" "III" and "IV," the most successful of the *Star Trek* films, and the popular Touchstone movie, "Three Men and a Baby." Most recently, he directed "The Good Mother" for Touchstone, which stars Diane Keaton and is set for an October release. Next month, he'll return to the bridge of the Starship Enterprise for "*Star Trek* V," which will be directed by castmate William Shatner.

The "*Star Trek* Adventure," which opened in June 1988, is a multi-million dollar participatory attraction which allows Tour visitors to star in a *Star Trek* featurette with the help of state-of-the-art special effects, detailed sets, and costumes designed by Robert Fletcher, wardrobe designer of the Paramount *Star Trek* films.

"The '*Star Trek* Adventure' is the very first attraction to incorporate all the different elements of television and motion picture production including instant editing, special effects, composite matting and filming, in a live theater

sets, and costumes

designed by Robert Fletcher, wardrobe designer of the

Paramount *Star Trek* films.

"The '*Star Trek* Adventure' is the very first attraction to

incorporate all the different elements of television and motion picture production including instant editing, special effects, composite

matting and filming, in a live theater event," said Phil Hettema, the show's producer. "In addition, the show lets our guests experience the fun of being a movie star."

I contacted the publicity department for Universal Studios upon learning of Nimoy's scheduled appearance and arranged to arrive early where I would gather with other journalists. We entered the building housing "The *Star Trek* Adventure" through a stage entrance. We took seats in a special section on the right front of the auditorium. We then waited while the rest of the audience entered. Then the same announcer who had been there for the June 9 grand opening came out on stage. He stated, "Hello, ladies and gentlemen! Welcome to the Star Trek Theatre at Universal Studios, Hollywood. I know many of you come to the studio wanting to be an actor or actress, and we have a special treat for you today, because not only are you going to get to meet an actor but also a chance to talk with him. Our special guest star today is a four time Emmy Award nominee! Not only is he an excellent actor, but also a very fine director, having directed last year's most successful mo-

tion picture, THREE MEN AND A BABY starring Tom Selleck, Steve Gutenberg and Ted Danson. He's also directed the movies *Star Trek* III and *Star Trek* IV, and the movie soon to be released starring Diane Keaton, and it's called THE GOOD MOTHER. Of course everyone knows him as Mr. Spock from the *Star Trek* television series and the *Star Trek* movies. Ladies and gentlemen, would you please welcome our very special guest star, Mr. Leonard Nimoy!"

Nimoy then walked out on stage greeted by thunderous applause.

"A very emotional bunch of humans," Nimoy observed.

"Hungry!" someone called out from the audience.

"Hungry?" he replied. "Are they supposed to feed you here? They're going to feed us Klingon meat, I think. It's not very good.

"Let me just start out by saying that your first question is probably what's happening next with *Star Trek*. As a matter of fact we start shooting *Star Trek* V in about ten days. The title is *Star Trek: The Final Adventure*. It will be released next summer. It is being directed by William Shatner. All of us will be there to help him out. So that's the answer to that question and I will expect you've got some others."

Someone in the audience asked how Nimoy got into the series IN SEARCH OF, which the questioner said was one of his favorite to watch when Nimoy was narrating.

"I was a very lucky guy," the actor replied. "They called me, and they said, 'Would you like to do this?' It was a series that had already been developed by the Alan Landsburg Company, and they were dealing with subjects that I was very interested in and that an audience would be and which would be dealing with searching for answers to the unknown, and they offered me the job. I said, yes, I would like to do that. I thought it would last for two or three years, but I think we did about eight years of those shows. It was a very successful show and I had a good time doing it. We filmed all around the world. I directed a few of them. I wrote a few of them. I could not be at all the places where all the filming was taking place because sometimes they'd have as many as five or six camera crews in different parts of the world filming different episodes, and I could not get to all of them. But I got to a number of them and, of course, I narrated all of them. I had a good time doing it."

The next question came from someone who directed her inquiry at "Mr. Spock" rather than at Leonard Nimoy. She asked him whether after traveling around the galaxy and visiting so many planets, Earth faced the only danger of polluting itself into extinction.

"You asked the question very well," he replied. "There's a charming humor in the way you asked the question, but the fact is that I happen to believe personally that we'd better do something about the environment on this planet very soon. When we were preparing *Star Trek* IV, I went around talking to a lot of scientists to develop the ideas for that movie. And one of the things that I asked them about were what were their concerns for the immediate future of this planet? A number of them told me that our society, not just this country

but this planet, has a tendency to assume that when a particular problem develops to the point where it's really getting serious (whether it be the ozone layer, pollution of the oceans or whatever) we say, okay, give the scientists all the money they want and they'll fix it. The scientists are saying that it may reach the point where they'll find that they'll have to say it's too late! You should've done this fifty years ago, or a hundred years ago! It's too late. We've reached the point of no return. So I'm concerned about that and I think we should all be watching for opportunities to protect this planet from ourselves."

A young boy asked Leonard how he did the whale scenes in *Star Trek* IV.

"That's a big question! How did we do the whale scenes in *Star Trek* IV? It's very complicated. I think a brilliant job was done by the special effects people and I really think they should have won an Academy Award. They were nominated, but they did not win, and I think the reason that they did not win was because the whales look so real. Most of the whale shots that you saw in *Star Trek* IV were miniatures about five feet long and they were radio controlled. Most of the whale footage was shot in a swimming pool in Marin County. They had a pool with a window that the radio operators could look through and see the whales inside. There'd be divers inside with cameras shooting footage. Outside the tank the operators were operating controls just like the radio controls on a remote controlled car. We also shot some scenes on the Paramount lot in a very large tank. The storm scene in San Francisco Bay with us hanging on to the ship while the whales swim by was shot there in a very large tank at Paramount.

"The deep underwater scene where Spock is doing the mind meld with the whale was shot at a McDonnell-Douglas NASA test tank down at El Segundo, California. So we picked up various pieces wherever we could get them done. The actual footage of actual whales only consisted of a couple shots when the whaling ship is actually chasing the whales near the end of the movie. There were a couple of shots of the whales roaring along the surface of the ocean. Those were actual shots that were filmed in Hawaii for us."

A young woman asked, "I'd like to know where Leonard leaves off and Mr. Spock starts, or where Mr. Spock leaves off and Leonard starts?"

"I'd like to know the answer to that question myself," Nimoy replied amid some laughter. "I've been living with this guy for a long time. How many of you here are under twenty-two? Well, those people weren't even born when we started doing *Star Trek*, and it was twenty-two years ago, in 1966, when it first went on the air." The audience applauded mention of that anniversary. "We thank you for your support for all these years. Believe me, we're very grateful.

"I like to believe that both Spock and I have changed in the process. I think that Spock was continually searching for an identity back through the Sixties and the Seventies, as many of us were, and so was I. I think as I have become more comfortable with myself, Spock has become more comfortable with himself. We really are quite different, nevertheless. I'm born on earth with an earth mother and an earth father and

Spock is not. I always enjoyed playing the differences. By that I mean I always thought that I was very lucky because I was cast to play a character who had great dignity. Great intelligence. Compassion. A sense of humor. I think we've changed together over the years. Another question?"

"Where are your ears?!" a little boy called out.

"They're out being sharpened," Nimoy quipped.

Then someone asked if they were ever going to bring *Star Trek* Classic in with *Star Trek: The Next Generation*.

"I don't know of any plans to do that specifically. I don't know of any plans to connect the two right now. I think right now the thinking is that that's the TV show and those are the movies. But anything is possible. We'll make this movie, number five, which shocks me. In the 1970's I never thought we'd make the first one. And then we did in 1979, which was almost ten years ago, and when that was done I thought, okay, now we've made the movie, so we're finished. And then we did *Star Trek* II and Spock died so I thought, okay, that's the end of that. But this thing keeps coming back and surprising me. I didn't expect that I would be in *Star Trek* III, and I ended up being both in it and directing it. And then came *Star Trek* IV and I had such a good time doing that, and now *Star Trek* V. And people keep asking me how many more of these am I going to do and the answer is, I don't know. I'll just keep on going as long as they want to do them."

Then someone asked Nimoy about the origin of the Vulcan hand salute.

"We once did an episode called 'Amok Time.' You probably know this better than I do. In 'Amok Time,' Spock going back to his planet for the first time in a long time, and he had been betrothed as a child, so he is going back to fulfill a marriage. And when he got to the planet, three of us, Kirk and Spock and McCoy, were beamed down to planet, and out from the city came this procession of Vulcans to meet us. They were the wedding party. And at the head of the procession, being carried in a sedan chair by some bearers, is this terrific matriarchal lady who was the head of the planet. Her name was T'Pau and she was played by a wonderful actress by the name of Celia Lovsky. So the scene is that she's saying hello to me and I'm supposed to say hello to her and she's supposed to say something like welcome home, Spock. But I was looking for some special kind of thing that we could do as Vulcans when we greet each other. So my point is that various kinds of people, races, whatever have some special kind of communication for each other. Some special kind of signal. Military people salute each other. Oriental people bow to each other. Eskimos rub noses with each other when they greet. So I thought, what do Vulcans do? And I thought back to my past and I remembered something. I was raised in an orthodox Jewish family. During the High Holy Days my parents would take me to the temple. There was a particular point in the service where the rabbi would bless the congregation with a prayer that's in both the old and the new testament, and when the rabbi did that the whole congregation would be standing. I would be with my father and I remember him saying to me,

'Don't look at the rabbi,' and everybody would turn away. I didn't know why, but I thought something very magical was going to happen while we're not looking. I heard them chanting this thing, and I remember being very furious. I was probably about eight years old, and what do you do when somebody says don't look? You sneak a peek! And I did, and what I saw when I turned was the rabbi doing this. (Nimoy holds out his hand in a way which looks like the Vulcan salute.) It's very magical. Every time I do that, flashbulbs go off. I was fascinated by it and I didn't know why he was doing that but I wanted to learn how to do it, and I practiced and it took me years of practice and self-denial. And I discovered later when I investigated that it was probably because this shape is the shape of what is a letter in the Hebrew alphabet which is the first letter in the Hebrew word for the almighty. So the idea is that the rabbi is probably using the letter signifying the Almighty's name when he blesses the congregation. So I learned how to do it and I thought this would be a good idea to use in *Star Trek* at this point so Vulcans could do that. I suggested it to the director, and he thought it was a nice idea, and he suggested it to the actress, and she said that it was fine with her, but there was a problem. The problem was that she had not spent the years of diligent practice and self-denial that I had, and she couldn't do it. She tried and came up with something really strange. But I thought that we've got to think of some way to get this done because I think it's going to be a really good show of the series. So what we did is that when you see the show you'll see that she's sitting in her chair

Stopped beside us was a very pretty young lady who looked over and recognized me, and she did that. (The Vulcan salute.) I got a kick out of that because we'd just gone on the air with that the previous week and here it's coming right back at me. I rolled down the window and asked her if she could do it with her left hand. She tried and got about that far and said, 'I speak it with an accent.' "

He then said there was time for a couple more questions. Someone asked him if he was interested in any other movie roles or if he was just going to be concentrating on directing.

"I'm having a pretty good time directing and I still would like to keep my hand in as an actor. And of course whenever a *Star Trek* project comes along I'll be there. I just finished directing a movie with Diane Keaton called THE GOOD MOTHER, which will be opening November 4th. It's very different from THREE MEN AND A BABY. It's a very serious film. I will be busy for the next thirteen, fourteen weeks acting in *Star Trek* V. Then I think I'd like to take a break because I've been working pretty steady without a break for the last four years or so. Maybe two or three months and then depending what comes along it will either be an acting job or a directing job."

Then someone asked him how he got into directing films.

"I was fiddling with direction for some time. I directed some stage work in the Fifties. I directed some television episodes in the Sixties and Seventies. I directed a T.J. HOOKER with William Shatner. And I directed a NIGHT GAL-LERY here at Universal. That was the very first film I did as a director. It was right here on this lot.

"When *Star Trek* II was finished and Spock had died, I thought that I was finished with *Star Trek*. I went to see the movie at a screening at Paramount for the entire cast and crew that made the film. We watched the movie and got down to the point where the ship is in trouble and we're about to be exploded and we can't get it going and Kirk yells down to the engine room, 'Scotty, I need warp speed in four minutes or we're all dead!' And there's no answer from the engine room. Spock hears this conversation and we see him get up out of his chair to go to the elevator and leave the bridge, and I know where he's going! He's going right down to the engine room to try to save the ship, and ends up dying in the process. I'm sitting there watching this and I was very moved by it. I thought it was very touching. Then at the very end of the movie, something I didn't expect. Spock's tube with his remains is fired out to the Genesis planet and now, something I didn't know was going to happen, the camera is on the planet panning through this leafy glen with a mist and so forth and comes to rest on this black tube containing Spock's remains. And I thought, oh, something's going to happen here! I think I'm going to get a call from Paramount pretty soon.

"They called me about a week later, and I went for a meeting and they said, 'We would like to know if you would like to be connected with the making of STAR TREK III in any way at all?' I said, yes, with all due respect to the people who've done these pictures, I've

Leonard Nimoy may have missed the premiere of the STAR TREK EXPERIENCE at Universal Studios but he was the star of his own show later that day.

been connected with Star Trek since 1966 and I think I could do as good a job directing as the other guys. I'd like to have a crack at it.' And that's how it all started. They gave me the job.

"When STAR TREK III was finished, before it opened, they called me and said, 'We'd like you to do another one.' And that's how STAR TREK IV happened. So that's how the directing all came about."

The final question came, "You've been on both sides of the coin as an actor and a director. When the script is performed in a rehearsal, and the actor disagrees with the director, who wins?"

"It depends on how big the actor is," Nimoy stated. "If you deal with Tom Selleck you've got to go a little slow.

Actually it's a very professional situation. You try to be collaborative. You try to let anybody who has an intelligent and professional point of view express themselves. Finally it is a director's responsibility to make the decision because he or she is supposed to have the overview of the entire project and how it should be shaped. The actors are there to make a contribution. Being an actor myself, I find it very useful to listen to actors and actresses because they often have very good ideas that I might not have thought of. They're playing the character. When I'm acting I appreciate a director who listens to me, and I try to do the same. I hope the product comes out better for it."

Music has always been a large part of the Star Trek experience, and the new TV series presents no exception.

Star Trek: The Next Generation's Music Composer

by Frank Garcia

When *Star Trek* television music is discussed, several composers come to mind. There's Alexander Courage, who composed the classic theme, and Fred Steiner, Sol Kaplan, Gerald Fried and Jerry Fielding. Now another name joins that very small list: Dennis McCarthy. He's the man responsible for merging the fanfare of the classic Courage TV theme with Jerry Goldsmith's *Star Trek: The Motion Picture* theme for *Star Trek: The Next Generation*.

McCarthy first became involved with Roddenberry and company when two producers of the show suggested him independently of each other. Bob Justman and Rick Berman, co-executive producers of the first season of the show, knew his work in composing music for *"V"* `and Paramount's *Mac-GYVER*. After submitting a sample tape of his music, he joined the show.

"Gene Roddenberry always loved the Jerry Goldsmith theme for *Star Trek: The Motion Picture*," explains McCarthy, explaining the origins of the *Next Generation* theme. "In talking with Rick Berman and Bob Justman, we all came to the idea, as a group, to

try using the Alexander Courage theme to start it out with. So I went home and turned on the horn section of the synthesizers and tried to put it together. It seemed to really fit the show, with the visuals of the ship warping off into space!"

That theme can now be heard along with the music score of the 2-hour pilot, "Encounter At Farpoint," on a recently released soundtrack album.

"What I'm going to do, and I think Neil Norman (producer of the album) would like to do also, is take excerpts from various shows and (each show is 22-25 minutes of music, some of them short cues) what I'd love to do is take the best cues (or music tracks) of each episode and make an album out of that. We'll re-record them so we won't have to spend a fortune paying the musicians to use their performance from each track (from different episodes)."

What McCarthy means when he says "re-recording the music" is that if he wants to use one music track each from, say, five episodes, then anyone who performed in that track has to be paid for their performance. Therefore he's paying for five times more than the economical *one* session performing those five tracks.

"I think we're trying to get something together as we speak," says McCarthy. "We're going to wait and see what comes out of the first couple of shows this season. We're using bigger orchestras, we're having 45 musicians next week which is unheard of in episodic television."

Discussing the creation of the soundtrack album, McCarthy says that "what happened with 'Farpoint' was that we had enough music from that one episode where we could go ahead and use the original soundtrack and create an album. It was quick. It only took us about two days to mix it.

"I loved 'Farpoint' because I just said, 'give me a tape, give me a studio and let's do it!' It was fun because when you do television, you can't spend three days doing one cue. You spend one day doing three shows!" laughs McCarthy. "You have the excitement of the immediate performance. A lot of the cuts on the soundtrack album were done in one take! Because of time, some of them were not even fully rehearsed! There just isn't time in television to sit around and have coffee and talk. . . It's 'hit it boys, and you're dead!'"

Is McCarthy pleased at the outcome?

"It's got energy. It's got life. I hear myself talking in the background!"

One of the unusual items contained in the album is an alternate theme never used in the show. It's one which had unpretentious beginnings.

"The alternate theme was only a re-

hearsal we happened to tape. It wasn't something planned. It was just, 'My gosh, we have 20 minutes! Let's just tape something here.' I wrote the theme for myself, for my internal use, to portray the Captain."

Many cast-members show a genuine interest. Jonathan Frakes, who plays Commander William Riker, has stopped by recording sessions to watch and see how the post-production end of the show is assembled.

Collector, special effects creator, model builder and current owner of one of three original Captain's chairs, Greg Stone parlayed his hobby into creatively contributing to Star Trek: The Next Generation.

Greg Stone

by C. J. Rivera

When the script calls for a certain well known British Secret Service Agent to fall into a pit teeming with hungry maggots, who do you call to conjure up the squirmy little devils and still have your actor available for your next movie?

Greg Stone.

When Starfleet officers become inhabited by a parasitical being who scurries around on six legs, is six inches long, and has long protruding mandibles, who do you call to manufacture, articulate and deliver these beasties all within nine days of the episode going on the air?

Greg Stone.

Greg Stone is fast becoming a rising star in the cosmos of special effects creations. He has created special effects for the James Bond movie, *License to Kill*, and the "Conspiracy" episode for *Star Trek: The Next Generation*. Greg works full time for a collections agency in Los Angeles. He first acquired his taste for science fiction from the original *Star Trek* episodes. After the show went off the air, he continued to cultivate his interest over the years, growing more and more fascinated by the

FX end of it.

In 1975 he helped Bjo Trimble with the construction of a bridge set for a *Star Trek* convention. At this convention (Equicon), Greg met Ralph Miller. Ralph shared a similar interest in *Star Trek* and special effects work. Together they teamed up to learn all they could about the subject. Eventually this led them into the special effects-model making end of their hobby. Together they created the a new company.

For the Trek episode "Conspiracy," Greg, with the help of his friend David Stipes, built 20 articulated parasite creatures and 50 non-articulated ones out of a special kind of foam rubber. Andrew Probert, Senior Graphic Illustrator for the first season of Star Trek: The Next Generation, created the original design of the creature. He got the assignment through a friend at a local FX shop. Taking a week off *from his job in Santa Ana, he p*ut together the effect which was to be in the film in 9 days! Not only was he able to pull it off in the short time given, but according to Richard Arnold, Official *Star Trek* archivist for Paramount, it was one of the more popular episodes of the first season. Richard said the studio received only six negative letters on that episode. The only negative reactions concerned the exploded half-torso at the end of the episode. Some thought it too graphically depicted on screen.

Greg is also a collector of *Star Trek* memorabilia. The pride and joy of his collection is one of three original captain's chairs from the original series which he acquired ten years ago. It sits in the corner of his living room rightfully adorned by *Star Trek* posters on the wall behind it. His collection also includes two of the original swivel chairs usually seen on the bridge, briefing room, or guest quarters. These seats, seen throughout the ship in the original series, were designed and built at the Brunswick company. The same company makes seats and lanes for bowling alleys throughout America. The chairs were custom made for the series with the incorporation of the swivel which, no matter where it was pointed, would always come back to the front. These chairs also had removable padded vinyl backs which slipped on and off. They also had vinyl cushions which slipped on and off when the occasion called for it. After the show's demise, these chairs appeared in Mrs. Brady's kitchen on the TV show *The Brady Bunch*.

The history of the Captain's chair, however, is a little darker. There were three chairs built during the entire production of the original series. The first chair is the one seen on the original pilot of "The Cage." As the story goes, when production of "The Cage" concluded, the sets went into storage. Later, when a second pilot began filming ("Where No Man Has Gone Before")

they needed another chair. The new one lasted through

There's a whole parallel world out there of fan activities including magazines, conferences, merchandise and clubs. Here's a road map...

Star Trek Fandom

by Scott Nance

David Gerrold is the author of old, animated, and new *Star Trek* scripts, including "The Trouble with Tribbles." In his book, *The World of Star Trek*, he writes what might begin to explain *Star Trek* fandom, "Trekkies have been compared with groupies. In one respect, the comparison is apt. Groupies follow rock stars around, hoping to share in the fame and magic of the super—star experience. Trekkies respond to *Star Trek* the same way——but much more intensely. In that respect, the comparison with groupies is unfair. For one thing, being a Trekkie involves a hell of a lot more work."

Star Trek fans consider their extra work labors of love. In the Sixties, fan Bjo Trimble began the tremendous task of organizing the letter—writing campaign that saved the original *Star Trek* for its third, and final, season. She had met *Star Trek* creator Gene Roddenberry early in the show's life and soon became "fan liaison" for the series, handling some of the show's fan mail.

Upon beginning the *Star Trek* letter writing campaign, Bjo got organized. College and high school newspapers spread the letter as did the Kansas City Star Tribune and the MENSA for Geniuses newsletter. Together they helped spread the word, and eventually NBC

received *over one million letters*! After the campaign, the network announced after the airing of an episode that, yes, the series would be back in the fall. This phenomenal achievement began *Star Trek* fan history. It was the first time fandom came together, in spirit if not in body. The show they loved.

Being a Trekkie——really serious fans call themselves "Trekkers" ——is a lot of work for Shirley Maiewski, the chairperson for the *Star Trek* Welcommittee, and all—around Trekker. "When *Star Trek* first came on, the Vietnam War was on, and there was a lot 'hidden' in the stories. There were a lot of things they were able to present in *Star Trek*, like having a black woman on the Enterprise. [Fandom] attracts thoughtful, deep—thinking people," said Shirley, talking about those who picked up on the show's "hidden" messages of hope for a peaceful future.

Her own work centers around co-ordinating the Welcommittee, which began in the early Seventies at the first *Star Trek* convention, held in New York City. Jacqueline Lichtenberg, one of the guests at that con, was somebody credited with knowing a lot about *Star Trek*, and she was getting many questions about the series in the mail. "That day [at the convention] Jackie asked me and some other people to help her with it," Shirley explained.

This became the *Star Trek* Welcommittee. The Welcommittee isn't a "fan club" Trekkers can join. It's a "resource organization" with representatives in the United States, Canada, England, Australia, Japan, and Brazil. It is one of the few fan organizations licensed by Paramount. When the studio receives *Star Trek* fan mail, often it is referred to the Welcommittee, a non-profit organization.

"If anyone has any question in any way related to *Star Trek*, they can write to us, and we'll try to find the answer," Shirley says, explaining the Welcommittee. "Because a lot of us are long—time fans we usually have some idea how to find it out. All we ask is that you send us a self—addressed, stamped envelope, and we'll do our best to answer it. We have many departments. If you want to start a club of your own, we have a pamphlet to help, or another about how to run a small convention."

Shirley says that most of the questions the Welcommittee receives come from fans interested in starting a club. Or from fans who want to know where and when the next conventions will take place or how fans can get involved with other fans. "There's the pen—pal department, of course. We publish a directory listing the *Star Trek* organizations we know of, plus books and the fanzines, dealers, actors' fan clubs, and just about anything you could think of related to *Star Trek*.

"We have other departments, as well. We have one woman in Germany. She coordinates [*Star Trek*'s] military fans around the world. We have about sixty—five people, most of whom are in the United States and Canada, but its really a world—wide thing. *Star Trek* has been shown in seventy-two different countries around the world," says Shirley, explaining the Welcommittee in more depth. The diversity and world—wide effect of *Star Trek*, the Welcommittee, and fandom in general, she adds, are reflections of each other.

Both *Star Trek* and its fan network are a huge world—wide phenomenon, a kind of global family. *Star Trek*, carrying its messages of world peace, diversity, and friendship, facilitates friendships in real life. "Someone can send in and we'll send them back a page or two of addresses of people who live near them, and then they'll write back [to us] and say, 'I've found so—and—so lives right around the corner or goes to my school, and I didn't know they were a *Star Trek* fan.' One benefit of being a fan is the friends you make, literally all around the world," says Shirley.

"It's college students and homemakers, and all kinds of people. We hear from all walks of life. When I first began, there were a great many college students [who where fans], and there still are. Now it's more scattered, I think. We get many youngsters. You can have an intelligent, interesting conversation with an eight year old—they call me 'Grandma Trek.'"

Conventions are like the family reunions of this global *Star Trek* family. General science fiction conventions have gone on for many years, but it wasn't until 1972 in New York that a group of people put together a *Star Trek* convention. This group was hoping for an attendance of 500, but they gave up counting after 2,000 fans showed up that weekend. Today, conventions, or "cons," are held on many weekends in a year, in many cities.

"Nice thing about a convention is you don't have to explain why you're there," says Shirley, because everyone there is a fan. There are really two kinds of cons, professional cons and fan cons. Professional conventions, like those run by Creation, attract thousands of fans and move to different cities on different weekends. Ultimately they reach most of the major cities in America. "Sometimes two or three a weekend in different parts of the country," Shirley said. It's through this kind of convention that people who don't live in New York or Los Angeles can experience a convention and meet actors and writers from the series.

Then there are the fan conventions, which Shirley calls, "The best kind." Shirley likes fan cons "best." Where a pro con opens at eleven in the morning and closes around six or seven at night, fan cons run almost twenty—four hours a day. Sometimes a fan con features an actor; sometimes it doesn't. A fan con usually offers a dealers' room, and sometimes a banquet, an art show, and a large array of panel discussions centered on *Star Trek*, all on the same agenda. Conventions are also a great place to see another creative fan outlet: costumes. Most cons offer masquerades where fans appear in meticulously sewn costumes. The handmade costumes often copying pre—designed patterns, sometimes creating their own. Fans—especially Spock fans— duplicate the make-up and appearance of their favorite *Star Trek* character. One handicapped Trekkie

came to the masquerade in his wheelchair as the crippled Captain Pike from the original series episode, "The Menagerie." Gene Roddenberry happened to be on hand that weekend and named that fan "Starfleet's first honorary admiral."

Some *Trek* conventions hope to earn a profit on the fan phenomenon, but most are celebrations of *Star Trek*, its world family, and the elements that make it special. As David Gerrold wrote, "Despite whatever else occurs at a *Star Trek* convention, the attendees have come because they are inspired by the show——and their actions demonstrate where their hearts are."

Unfortunately, cons last only a weekend. *Star Trek* fans want to keep their love alive year 'round, so they write. They write pen-pal letters, as noted above, and beyond that—despite the new stories presented on television and in theatres—fans write their own stories. In fact they fill reams of paper, thousands of magazines, with stories of their favorite *Star Trek* characters.

Fan written and published stories range from deadly serious adventures in which key characters meet their final fate to tongue-in-cheek tales loaded with bad puns.

One large group of stories by fans involes the characters in sexual encounters, often fulfilling fantasies of the writers themselves. These pornographic stories cover quite a range of sexual taboos. Some even involve a relationship between Kirk and Spock never considered in *Star Trek* proper.

Several of the writers who begin with fan fiction go on to professional writing careers.

Transforming a movie into a novel is always a tricky business. How well did the Star Trek novels work?

Comparison: Movies and Novels

by Scott Nance

Many blockbuster movies owe their inspiration to books. In the case of *Star Trek*, however, the movie and the book were usually produced at roughly the same time. *Star Trek* creator Gene Roddenberry wrote the novelization of Alan Dean Foster's story, *Star Trek: The Motion Picture*. Then, prominent science—fiction and *Star Trek* writer Vonda McIntyre followed with novelizations of *The Wrath of Khan, The Search for Spock*, and *The Voyage Home*. Finally, J.M. Dillard, the writer of Pocket Books *Star Trek* novelizations *Bloodthirst and Demons*, wrote the adaptation of *Star Trek V: The Final Frontier*. These writers adapted the different movies with varying outcomes.

Gene Roddenberry did *Star Trek: The Motion Picture* more than justice with his book. Roddenberry's novel enhanced *ST:TMP* by clarifying several points ambiguous in the movie. He added characterization and plot elements lacking in a film largely occupied with special effects and not storytelling. The original TV show rendered special effects secondary because they were too expensive. This weakness in the original show shifted the emphasis to plot and character.

In contrast, the first movie played down plot and character in order to show off more effects. *Star Trek: The Motion Picture* tried to ride the *Star Wars* wave of the late Seventies, so Paramount emphasized special effects. As a result, the first *Star Trek* movie was considered slow and plodding. The fans wanted more characterization and plot detail concerning the regular Enterprise crew. They asked why Spock chose the Kolinahr and emotionally gave up on his friends, as well as details concerning the short—lived introductions to the crew, Commander Decker and Lt. Ilia. They wanted more specifics about Ilia's Deltan race, and the man whom Kirk recommended to take his place aboard the Enterprise.

In his book, Gene Roddenberry fills in these gaps and adds other nuances, making the novel a hand—in—hand companion to the movie. Roddenberry fleshes out Ilia and Decker, and probes deeply into Kirk's psyche, especially his need to regain the Enterprise. He touches on the old crew's inner confusion and distress at Spock's newfound detachment and aloofness from them. He writes that even after Spock joins

85

them and the "old crew" is reunited, it's still not the "good ol' days" of the original mission. Roddenberry illuminates Kirk's troubles with Admiral Nogura that led to his loss of the Enterprise. He also details Kirk's relationship with Admiral Lori Ciana. J.M. Dillard later expounded on this in the novel, *The Lost Years*.

Compared to the book, the movie plods, but reading the book makes *Star Trek: The Motion Picture* better with repeated viewings.

Where Roddenberry added nuances, Vonda McIntyre added entire dimensions in her novels of *Star Trek II, III* and *IV*. After the first movie, Paramount complained about the final budget coming in at $40 million. They blamed Gene Roddenberry and removed him as producer. Paramount's handed the project to their more economical TV department and Harve Bennett. Among other shows, Bennett had previously produced TV's *Six Million Dollar Man*.

Bennett's aim was to return *Star Trek* to its roots. He realized action stories and three dimensional, full—blown, interacting characters made the original television series great. To capture the magic of the original series, he watched every episode. Then he based *Star Trek II* on "Space Seed," returning the evil Khan Noonian Singh. Ricardo Montalban again played the villain. Admiral Kirk's reunion with Khan fit what Bennett saw as *Star Trek*.

Like the first movie, the special effects in *Star Trek II: The Wrath of Khan* is superb. The wonderful space battles in a beautiful nebula still allow the actors time to *act*. The characters come alive,

with stronger resemblance to the original series. The old spirit of the Enterprise and her crew also returns and Kirk comes through in the nick of time. Like the original series, *Star Trek II* presents the struggles of real human life, in this case Spock's tearful, and well—acted, demise. Special effects and storytelling combine to good effect and neither steals the show.

Vonda McIntyre's captures the fast—paced story and offers beautiful characterization in her novelization of *Star Trek II*. She combines the swiftness of the movie with internal thoughts of the characters impossible to express on screen. She also includes many scenes that the film-makers simply did not have time to present. She creates a dispute between Lt. Saavik and Kirk about the Kobayashi Maru simulation that adds layers to Saavik's character. It's through the book that we really get to know Saavik and her life well. McIntyre includes a new scene at the end of the book. Spock is dead and Saavik sits through the night in the stasis room keeping her own personal watch over his body. As she makes this last gesture, she recalls her experiences with near-death on her own brutal home world.

The Genesis research team becomes much more detailed and two Deltan characters are added to the story. The dramatic scene in the Genesis station —when Khan demands the Genesis formula and eventually murders the research team— makes the later scene — when Kirk and company come to find most of the Genesis team hanged— all the more painful. In the movie, we don't meet any Genesis workers except the Marcuses, but in the novel we get to know and like the team, which makes the Genesis murders even more traumatic.

McIntyre has used her talents to create an exceptional novel based on an exceptional movie. The characters in the movie are bright and alive. Good and evil are painted in living strokes. McIntyre reflects this in the book, keeping the flavor of the screenplay, but adding scenes to enhance the story.

Trek fans were in suspense in 1984 as to Spock's future (if any) as *Star Trek III: The Search For Spock* saw released. Many were also curious, since Leonard Nimoy was definitely coming back, as director! That this was the first time a cast member directed a *Trek* production added to the excitement. In interviews, the actors were generally supportive of Nimoy's directorial work.

Star Trek II had no connection to the first motion picture. However, in telling the story of Spock's return, *Star Trek III* picked up where *The Wrath of Khan* left off. In its "search for Spock," *Star Trek III* went in a different direction than *The Wrath of Khan. Star Trek II*'s good guy versus bad guy scenario pitting Kirk against Khan resembles *Star Wars*. Like the best series episodes, *The Search for Spock* doesn't simply restrict itself to good versus evil. It was a more intelligent look at human nature in the style that makes *Star Trek* work so well.

The original series was exciting, but there were deeper questions of good and bad in *Star Trek* than in other space adventures of the day. Similarly, the Klingon confrontation in *Search for Spock* was a necessary plot device and added to the excitement. Yet the main

storyline was about more than hero and villain. Most of the film dealt with human fallibility. David selfishly used the destructive protomatter heedless of the cost; the Enterprise crew disobeyed orders leading to the destruction of the Enterprise, and determined to save Spock and McCoy. This made the characters more human than in the other movies. The Klingons, notably Kruge, become more than just Klingon villains, but real people. Not humans, but individuals with conflicting thoughts and desires.

Vonda McIntyre followed the direction of the movie when Paramount again recruited her to pen the novelization. Without altering the original words of the screenplay, she added to the reader's appreciation of the story. The wake for Spock that opens the novel drives home the realization that Spock is dead. We see the crew deal with the pain before rushing off in hopes of rescuing Spock. McIntyre continues the life of Carol Marcus, who never reappeared on screen after the end of the second movie. She has to deal with her research team's death, and re-examines her relationship with Jim Kirk. McIntyre also includes scenes of a love relationship between David Marcus and Saavik.

Star Trek IV: The Voyage Home finishes a trilogy that began with *Star Trek II*. Each of the segments in the trilogy unfolds a story that returns the premise to its incomparable magic of the Sixties. The second movie brought the characters back to the identifiable people that we know and love. The third movie returned the "feel" of an episode by raising complex questions of life. The fourth movie best returned to the roots of the original series. The Voyage Home proved the worth of the adage "everything in moderation." The series juggled many elements including believable characters, strong story, and prudently used special effects while addressing something important. The fourth movie followed the established formulae in the best way possible. It made us laugh, cry, hope, and think.

Vonda McIntyre's final adaptation of a Star Trek movie was of The Voyage Home. She continued to add scenes missing from the movie, but this time she also altered scenes already established by the screenplay. Although she hoped to add detail, when she altered the words of the characters, she changed the original story. This is particularly noticeable if you read the book after seeing the movie. McIntyre's expansion to the story works when she adds her own scenes, but when she starts altering the scenes already created by the movie, her story no longer works.

Star Trek V: The Final Frontier seemed almost anti-climactic after the "Genesis story" in Star Trek II and III and the resolution in The Voyage Home. While actor-turned-director Nimoy deftly guided the last two adventures by searching for Star Trek's essence, William Shatner failed.

Nimoy put together the components that made Star Trek special, taking advantage of the extra time allowed by the movie format to highlight regular supporting cast. Shatner, on the other hand, reversed direction completely in Star Trek V. He made Kirk central, shutting the other characters out. Where Nimoy brought the supporting regulars out of the scenery, Shatner

pushed them back into the role of props they usually were in the series. Shatner's story was a good idea that grew ponderous. The previous three movies—especially those filmed by Nimoy— used different aspects of classic Star Trek: characters, story, special effects. The Final Frontier, on the other hand, was cluttered with different subplots and themes.

J.M. Dillard in her novelization did the best to make sense out of the clutter. In Vonda McIntyre's style, Dillard added a prologue in the book which constituted scenes not in the movie. In this prologue, we meet Sybok, Spock's stepbrother who suddenly appears after all these years, as a boy. We also meet his mother T'Rea, a Vulcan High Master stripped of her position by her heresy. She speaks of a promised heaven, Sha Ka Ree, a crusade later taken up by her son. This, of course, makes up the main plot of The Final Frontier. Dillard also explores the social make-up of Nimbus III, the "Planet of Galactic Peace" by revealing J'Onn in more depth. Her additions, like those Roddenberry wrote into his adaptation of the first movie, occur less frequently than those of McIntyre.

Although Dillard made a valiant attempt, she could not completely fill in all the gaps and organize the plot enough to save the story. Too many things must fit— the discovery of Spock's brother, hostile Klingons and Romulans who at the end of the story hold a cocktail party with the Enterprise crew, the broken world of Nimbus III and its rag—tag inhabitants, and a meeting with a God—creature. All must be fit into two hours and three hundred pages. *The various parts of the*

Walter Koenig continued to play a major role in all four movies, with perhaps his most dramatic scenes coming in THE WRATH OF KHAN.

movie were off—balance and failed to ring true to the familiar ideals of the original show. *The Final Frontier,* in its own way, also failed.

Rumor has it that the original crew will stop making mov*ies after Star Trek VI.* A lot will be riding on *VI,* with the ups and downs of the other movies under consideration. The five previously released films worked when they took elements of the series and combined them with a message of humanity.

Many ships have carried the proud name Enterprise. These two crews manned a starship for the Federation

Two Generations of Trek

by Scott Nance

Before *Star Trek: The Next Generation* premiered, speculation ran wild. Would it continue where *Star Trek IV* left off, presenting weekly adventures of William Shatner, Leonard Nimoy and the others? Would it be new actors playing Kirk, Spock, McCoy, and the rest of the crew?

Of course what came to pass was new characters played by a different cast. Fan reaction split, some praising the innovations and new directions, others damning the interloper.

The Next Generation premiered with the two hour pilot, "Encounter at Farpoint." This episode clearly defined the crew of the Galaxy class NCC-1701-D, USS Enterprise. It also showed they were going to "go boldly where no one has gone before." The commander of the ship is a Frenchman, Captain Jean-Luc Picard, a man in his mid-fifties, and obviously a highly-valued Starfleet officer.

In many ways, he is James Kirk's equal. From what we learn about Picard, he has commanded some of the most challenging missions ever conducted. Everyone takes his abilities seriously, as seriously as he takes his assignments. Picard has a sense of humor, but it seems in a more "classical" sense. He is closer to the James

Kirk we see in the later movies, more seasoned, less brash. He knows several Starfleet Admirals on a first-name basis. Unlike Kirk, Picard, although promotable material, fended off those who would have stuck him planet-bound as an admiral. He has continued to do what he loves, commanding a starship.

Picard is a much more formal officer than Kirk, however. Where James Kirk had a close camaraderie with his crew, even becoming quite close to several of them, Picard maintains a working relationship, but allows nothing more. He has made it abundantly clear he doesn't like dealing with the children aboard his ship, delegating that duty to his "number one," First Officer Riker.

William T. Riker is a good-looking man, who makes a good commander and works well under Picard's authority. He is more like the Kirk of the original series, intelligent, yet brash. He displays none of Picard's formality. Starship captains no longer usually lead landing parties, now called "away teams." The first officer leads instead. Riker possesses the youthful charisma of a Kirk. Like Kirk, Riker has developed genuine friendships with various crewmembers who serve under him. This closeness inspires the crew's loyalty as it did for James Kirk. On the away team he commands, Riker is firm as Kirk when the situation calls for it while also possessing a superb diplomatic skill, which enhances Picard's own prowess in this area.

Commander Deanna Troi represents both a new race and a new position aboard a starship. Troi, half Betazoid and half human is the ship's "counselsor." Aboard ship she acts as a "ship's psychologist," especially for the command crew, and planetside she advises her captain in contacts with outsiders. Troi, as all Betazoids, is an empath. She can "sense" emotions from those she is in contact with, either in person or over visual communication systems. Unlike a telepath, Betazoids cannot read thoughts, just emotions. Troi is one of the *Next Generation* crewmembers that fans have scrutinized most. 'What real purpose does she serve?' fans ask. Many times the situation arises where "hostiles" are pointing a gun at the Starfleet officers and she "senses" these hostiles are "angry." It seems a little obvious. Other times, however, as in the episode "Justice," Troi brings hidden emotions to light for her captain, aiding in his decision making.

The actress who plays Troi, Marina Sirtis, is talented, it just seems that the scriptwriters need to learn how to use her character more evenly. Her sensitivity, caring, and intelligence give her great potential if the writers put her empathic powers to definite use.

The other alien aboard ship is Lieutenant Worf, a Klingon serving aboard a Federation starship. By the time of *The Next Generation*, the "great friendship" between the Federation and Klingon Empire the Organians spoke of has finally coming to pass.

Worf is a powerful member of the crew, one of the strongest, not only physically, but also in terms of story. Worf, like the others, has powerful convictions and is highly respectful of the crew. We finally see a totally whole Klingon, rather than a slimy "bad guy" or caricature of evil.

Worf reminds me of Spock. While Troi is a Betazoid, outwardly she appears human. Worf, like Spock, "looks" alien. This sets him apart from the others. Worf carries an air of mystery, like Spock. He is fiercely proud of his heritage, but has a deep desire to "fit in." There is much to be cultivated in the future.

Lieutenant Commander Data, however, has been the obvious "Spock-comparison" on *The Next Generation*. He follows Riker in command, and is unemotional like Spock. Data is an "alien" in his own way. He isn't human, but also isn't a stoic Vulcan. Data is an android serving aboard the Enterprise. With his computer brain, it is Data spouting exacting details to the captain, where Spock had served that role previously. There are many differences that outweigh the minor similarities. Data is not trying to hide emotion. On the contrary, he is trying to cultivate it.

Data is an interesting character because he is trying very hard to become more human. He has a great sense of wonder, especially about things human. Through this process, we see a lot about ourselves as humans from this wonder-of-an-outsider point-of-view. This makes Data more human than anyone else, which is one of the best elements explored in the new series.

Security chief lieutenant Tasha Yar, until her demise in the episode "Skin of Evil," was another strong character. She represents one of the triumphs of this new series, a woman in a position of power. Gene Roddenberry has always tried to innovate ways of seeing people. At the time of the original series, having Uhura, a black woman, helping run the ship was quite an achievement. Unfortunately, due to budget and network constraints, Uhura rarely emerged from the background to promote an appreciation of diversity.

Now in the Eighties, without the constraint of a network, Roddenberry gives us a powerful, intelligent woman. She heads a department and is taken very seriously, accorded respect, admiration, and friendship by those who serve with her. Unlike Uhura, Yar became more than a "hailing frequency opener." Where there was never an established security officer in the original series, Yar put a human face on this "spear-carrier" role. Her character added to the plots of the show and the success of the new series.

Besides this symbol for equality and diversity, Yar was an interesting character. She grew up on a savage world, spending her childhood avoiding rape gangs. After her rescue, she entered Starfleet. These experiences toughened her, yet she remained strongly compassionate. Denise Crosby created an interesting multi-faceted character in this role.

Chief Medical Officer Leonard "Bones" McCoy played an important part in the original series. The emotional, caring "ol' country doctor" is often compared to the new Enterprise's chief medical officer. The Next Generation have been served thus far by two chief medical officers. In the first season, Dr. Beverly Crusher appeared as a very competent and caring physician like McCoy. Beverly seemed more eager to use advanced medical technology than Bones was. Where Bones served as the ship's psychologist and as a major presence in command decisions, Beverly did very little of either. She had a strong dedication to medicine, but didn't go much farther.

Dr. Crusher left the Enterprise during the second season in order to take an Earth-side assignment, although she returned for the third season. In the interim, Dr. Katherine Pulaski replaced her. Diana Muldaur, who played two guest roles in the first series, appearing as Miranda Jones and Lt. Ann Mulhall, finally filled a somewhat regular part.

Pulaski is a curmudgeon, and in that way, more like Bones McCoy. She exchanged barbs with Data, stepping dangerously close to a Bones-Spock-type feud. It seems as if she was written to be a "Bones replacement," which didn't work. Given more time to develop her own personality, she could have been a worthwhile addition to the crew.

Beverly Crusher is a widow who has a son, Wesley, aboard with her. While Riker resembles the Kirk of the original series, Wesley Crusher reflects a young James Kirk. Like Kirk, Wesley can be too cute for his own good, but also has a determination to succeed. Also, Wesley is Gene Roddenberry's middle name and is probably Roddenberry's mixture of what his boyhood was and what he wanted it to be. Wesley is shy, intelligent, and friendly. He's still trying to figure out the galaxy, not just the academic stuff, but the social realm as well.

Despite his "cuteness," Wesley gives us another perspective we have seen little of before in *Star Trek,* that of a young person. It would be nice if the writers—as they have done in various episodes— toned down Wesley's cute aspects. They could instead show more of the life of a young person of the future.

The last regular character in *The Next Generation* is an officer who has helped Wesley along quite a bit. Lieutenant Geordi LaForge started the first season as the helmsman then moved to the engine room as chief engineer. LaForge also strikes a blow for diversity. He is a blind man who piloted the ship. He sees through a prosthetic device which gives him quite a range of sight into the ultraviolet and infrared ranges. With Geordi, *Star Trek* demonstrates that disabled people can make valuable contributions if given the chance.

Geordi is the young adventurous one who emotionally resembles Sulu. He is an intelligent, yet playful and exciting member of the crew. LaVar Burton's portrayal of Mr. LaForge is one of the best in the show, especially in putting across youthful enthusiasm for the adventures the Enterprise embarks upon. Like Sulu, LaForge comes through in a pinch, but also helps keep things light when necessary.

Despite initial hesitation as to whether *The Next Generation* was "real *Star Trek,*" fans became supportive. Ratings and Paramount's support of the show almost guarantee a five year run.

What works best about the show is the key voice behind the camera: Gene Roddenberry. He took the original concept behind *Star Trek* and expanded it. The luxury of having a successful *Star*

Trek rather than one continually in danger of cancellation has given Roddenberry the opportunity to "fix mistakes" of the original show.

Women gain more authority and respect aboard this new Enterprise. Three of the main characters are women: Troi, Dr. Crusher, and, in the first season, Tasha Yar. In the old series, we had only Uhura and later Chapel, although Uhura murmured "I'm frightened" and Chapel's primary duty was to moon over Spock. As Roddenberry has said in the past, he built the original series upon compromises with the network. Because of these compromises, he couldn't bring all the his ideas to the screen. In the original pilot for the first series, "The Cage," Roddenberry had a female first officer, "Number One" and an alien, Spock. The network felt that they had to go; that the TV audience couldn't accept them. Roddenberry compromised and kept Spock, the Vulcan alien. Now with *Star Trek* as successful as it is, and since Paramount is syndicating the new show itself with no network, Roddenberry has faced fewer compromises.

Another fixed "mistake" is the use of the captain. Realistically, the captain and the first officer should not both leave the ship and be fired at by aliens week after week. The powers that be at the time of the original series wanted to get all they could out of the attractive leading man, William Shatner. They wanted him included in as many scenes as possible.

In *The Next Generation*, Captain Picard rarely leaves his ship, and then only after one of First Officer Riker's away teams has secured the area. Also, Kirk was unrealistically young to be commanding such a large vessel in the original series. Picard is somewhat older, a more seasoned officer for so demanding a mission as deep-space exploration.

Like the original series, *The Next Generation* has its faults and its own weak stories. The new series also possesses brilliant triumphs, unforgettable moments, and stories that illuminate the condition of humanity.

This new series enjoys a split relationship with the original. It carries the *Star Trek* name, and the Gene Roddenberry bestowed promise of greatness. On the other hand, the characters possess unique personalities, and must be looked at separately.

The new crew of the Enterprise will continue to go boldly where no one has gone before, but in their own direction.

The second STAR TREK outing may still rank as the best of all the feature films....

LOOKING BACK THE WRATH OF KHAN

by Al Christensen

"It is a far, far better thing that I do, than I have ever done;

it is a far far better rest that I go to, than I have ever known."

-Sydney Carton before the guillotine in *A Tale of Two Cities*.

Star Trek II: The Wrath of Khan is generally contended to be better, in almost every respect, than the first *Star Trek* film. There was critical support from unexpected quarters outside fandom; mainstream reviewers from newspapers, magazines and TV, who felt obligated in many instances to identify themselves as "non-Trekkies" and had little sympathy for *Star Trek: The Motion Picture*, wrote largely receptive reviews for *The Wrath of Khan*.

The reaction of Trek fans, on the other hand, who were twice shy after being once bitten, seems to be one more of a relief than ecstasy. No, Harve Bennett and Nick Meyer didn't goof it up, at least not glaringly. No parade of awe-struck reaction shots. No cathedral rec-rooms. No overwrought vision of special effects. Small is beautiful. The lighting is less flat and pervasive. There are shades to hide in, where

monsters of Id can strike from, just as in the early episodes on TV. The acting is more relaxed and there is a homey camaraderie again. No ambition to be another earthshaking 2001, just good entertainment like *Forbidden Planet*. *The Wrath of Khan pretty* much accomplishes its aims. But is gratitude overextending itself?

The Wrath of Khan remains true to the principles of *Star Trek* and manages to be diverting as well. It is an important contribution to the universe of Trek since it introduces new variables, like Lt. Saavik and Kirk's son, and phases out old ones, like Khan Noonian Singh and Mr. Spock - if only temporarily. But as a movie seen through non-fan eyes, Khan is somewhat of an anachronistic action picture. It is science fiction used to tell a story which has outlived its time.

Just as *Blade Runner* is essentially Forties film noir, *Raiders of the Lost Ark* and *Star Wars* Saturday matinee derring-do and *E.T.* Disney reborn, *The Wrath of Khan* is eighteenth-century naval warfare reminiscent of Horatio Hornblower. Broadsides in space (though to surprisingly feeble effect), Khan and his cohorts looking and act-

95

ing like pirates, chess-like military stratagems and death and destruction. Star Fleet uniforms appear to be un-ostentatious designs by Napoleon's tailor. All this is evidence of an underlying texture of iron men and wooden ships, a subliminal *Damn the Defiant*.

Star Trek, however, isn't a stranger to such seafaring tactics. As a TV series it hosted an episode titled "Balance of Terror" in which the Enterprise tries to prevent a raiding Romulan vessel from returning to its base. In actuality the episode is an uncredited remake of a World War Two movie with Curt Jurgens and Robert Mitchum playing a cat-and-mouse game in the Atlantic between an American destroyer and a German submarine; the movie was *The Enemy Below*.

The anachronisms don't stop there.

Nicholas Meyer, *Star Trek II: The Wrath of Khan*'s director, has a fascination for past eras. One can see the care and research behind his film *Time After Time*, a tale of two ages in which H.G. Wells goes forward in time on a manhunt for Jack the Ripper. Meyer also wrote the script for the well-received TV movie *The Night That Panicked America*, a dramatization of the effects Orson Welles' radio version of "The War Of The Worlds" had on a nation one Halloween. But Meyer's antiquarian bent is in full view in two successful novels he authored (or "edited" for "John H. Watson, M.D."), *The Seven Percent Solution* and *The West End Horror*, both adventures of that other creature of ratiocination, Sherlock Holmes. Famous personalities and events of a Victorian age, everything from Sigmund Freud and Oscar Wilde to circumstances that led up to World

War One, were drawn upon for the books; Conan Doyle would probably appreciate their faithfulness.

Similarly, Meyer has left his mark on *Star Trek II: The Wrath of Khan*. Admiral Kirk seems a reflection of the director's idiosyncrasy; Kirk is a collector, his apartment a museum of antique artifacts of which some are conspicuously of martial origin. The glasses Dr. McCoy gives him adds to this image while emphasizing the Admiral's self-doubts and fears of advancing age. On Ceti Alpha 5, the library of the exiled Khan partially consists of *Moby Dick, Paradise Lost* and *Dante's Inferno*; Khan himself seems an amalgam of malevolent intentions from these classics. In the "Space Seed" episode, Khan was a eugenic superman, and because "superior ability breeds superior ambition," he was banished from Earth after an attempt at world domination. Freed from hibernation by Captain Kirk, Khan then tries to take over the Enterprise only to be subdued. Given a choice between rehabilitation or exile, Khan answers that it is "better to rule in Hell than to serve in Heaven." In Meyer's *Star Trek II* Khan has changed. His superior ambition has become a Captain Ahab obsession, fanned into unremitting hatred for Admiral Kirk by the death of his wife (I'm sorry, Mr. Shatner, but you're the great white whale.) Even more basic than this, however, is Khan's contempt for the established morality system; like the Fallen Angel of *Paradise Lost*, he wants to establish his own order.

In this respect, Khan's motivations roughly correspond to those of Jack the Ripper in *Time After Time*, who found the morally bankrupt twentieth century a playground compared to his own straight-laced age; Khan's crimes, though committed more out of expedience than of malice, are no less gruesome and spine-chilling. Kirk as a galactic policeman proved the strength of his ethical system by recapturing Khan and exiling him to Ceti Alpha 5; by removing Kirk, Khan would confirm his assertion of god-like superiority: "Improve Man and you gain a thousandfold." At the moment before the villain, physically broken and on the verge of defeat, unleashes the power of the Genesis Device in a desperate attempt to destroy his nemesis though it means his own end, the scene conjures up a Miltonesque tableau with ornate monologue delivered with defiantly Luciferian hubris by Ricardo Mantalban--a devil spitting in the eye of the Master.

Meyer appears to have had a great deal of input in *Star Trek II*. In testimony, Jack B. Soward, the screenwriter, indicated that much of his script was changed. In a *Starlog* magazine interview he stated< "I invested Khan with certain powers. He could make you see things which didn't actually exist. When Khan arrives, he gestures at David (Kirk's son), who rolls up in a ball of pain. Kirk tells David, It's all in your mind, David. None of this is happening; FIGHT it. Suddenly Kirk and Khan appear on a beach, armed with these scorpion-tipped Romulan whips. They fight with those to the point where Kirk is almost beaten. Then Khan shifts them to a desert, where with new weapons, Khan beats the sh-t out of Kirk once again, inflicting terrible punishment."

According to the interview, the se-quence described was in the final draft of the script the writer submitted. Sowards must have known that the powers attributed to Khan would be inconsistent with the character's past which demonstrated no such mental prowess. Apparently it occurred to someone else and the sequence was deleted. Further, the sequence is a visual cliche from the days of the *Flash Gordon* serial and their heyday of the TV action show, where every fifteen minutes a prolonged, choreographed fistfight broke out, often to tiresome effect. What is distressing, too, is Soward's attitude towards *Star Trek*: "It's a western set in a different place." The writer's remarks seem curiously out-of-place when confronted with the multi-layered quality of *Star Trek II: The Wrath of Khan*'s story.

Whoever is responsible for the final product, there is a definite literary allusion running through the film. *The Wrath of Khan* has much in common, thematically, with Dickens' *A Tale of Two Cities*. "The needs of the many outweigh the needs of the few," Spock tells Kirk. True to his word, the Vulcan gives his life to save the Enterprise and the lives of David, his mother, and the Admiral. In *A Tale of Two Cities*, Sydney Carton takes the place of the sentenced Charles Darnay at the guillotine in order that Darnay, his wife, and father-in-law may escape the horrors of the French Revolution. Carton dies to redeem a life, his own, which he feels has been misspent; Spock sacrifices himself out of unspoken bonds. Both are destined to serve a high purpose. "It was the best of times, it was the worst of times," reads the beginning of Spock's gift to Kirk; the yin-yang sentiment expresses the duality of Kirk's melancholy, that while he has risen in importance and responsibility commensurate with advancing age, he has been promoted out of that when he loved the most. The Dickens quote can also encompass in a subtler way the nature of the Genesis Device. A force which can change a barren planetoid or starship into a life-bearing world with a sun (the how of it is more alchemical than scientific) in a matter of seconds represents remarkable progress, but at the same time it can be a force of immense destruction, destroying life to create life. The Genesis Device seems a metaphor for the rampant technological change of the present that brings new hope for those who can meet its challenge, but leaves behind in its wake those who cannot.

Lt. Saavik may have been, at first, a female Spock surrogate; in fact, the older half-alien visibly treats her as an understudy, grooming her for a starship command (this sort of semi-nepotism abounds in *Star Trek I*: Khan and the sensible Joachim, Scotty and his nephew--a kinship excised from the movie--played by Ike Eisenmann, and of course, Kirk and David). It's apparent, however, that Saavik has a mind of her own. She has an impish sensuality that is barely suppressed and, for a member of a pointy-eared race that doesn't put much stock in displays of emotion, she is very spirited. Some point to Saavik's visible grief at Spock's funeral as a flaw in the film, but for what is perhaps the most manipulative scene in the movie, some response seems reasonable. Even Mr. Spock would not have been likable if he were completely stoic. In the "Menagerie" episode which in-

cluded the first pilot with Jeffery Hunter, Number one, the archetype for both Spock and Saavik, and played by Majel Barrett, was a real cold fish - a cross between a computer and a woman. She was cut from the series due to a cool reception by network executives, her aloofness transferred to the then sketchy character of Mr. Spock (hear the phonograph album, Inside Star Trek"). Kirstie Alley appears to have overcome many of the same barriers that Number One faced, but without being emasculating or overbearing. Saavik's background is only hinted at; however, partisans already want to know more. It would be fascinating to see how Lt. Saavik relates to sexism and the views of Terran women.

Saavik's youth brings up again Kirk's traumatizing menopause and perhaps that of *Star Trek* as a whole. The Admiral refuses to face his own mortality or even the passing years. *Star Trek* itself is a struggle against entropy, attempting to live up to expectations predicted by nostalgia of its followers. They would, naturally, never consider a Kobiashi Maru scenario for their project of adoration. The film forced the audience to confront the mortality of the mythos by ostensibly killing off the entire bridge crew in the opening sequence, except new-comer Saavik. The production staff must have gotten some satisfaction from this scene after the way certain vocal detractors had raked them over the coals during the Spock death brouhaha. While *Star Trek II* doesn't exactly rejuvenate the not-so-timeless concept, Meyer and company do perpetuate *Star Trek* as an artifact of popular culture, susceptible to disappearing tomorrow. *Star Trek* is not art, as *Star Trek: The Motion Picture* tried to disprove; *Star Trek II: The Wrath of Khan* views itself as something-less-than-greatness-for-the-ages and accepts it.

Originally, in the pre-production phase, the Star Trek sequel was intended as a TV movie. This accounts for *Star Trek II: The Wrath of Khan*'s cathode-screen flavor, not all of it the intrinsic nature of the space opera. Largely it is the subjective reflection of how the film-makers saw Star Trek as a television series. Anachronistic, parochial, militaristic and pseudo-scientific- perceptions that are slightly right of center but close enough to the bullseye as not to be aggravating - *Star Trek I* could well have been an introspection of the mystique of *Star Trek* itself. The storyline internalized; a quasi-Greek tragedy almost without allegorical threads. The interdependency of the characters is nearly the entire story, the Genesis Device being the only element which speaks to the immediacy of the socio-political present. This was a reversal of how it was done in the television series; until the third season, it was the idea that dominated the story with human conflicts arising from the consequences. *Star Trek: The Motion Picture* was also presented in this fashion. In *The Wrath of Khan*, the "no-win" situation, David's antagonism, Khan's obsession, etc, revolve around Kirk's angst to Freudian intricacy. The Genesis Device was a convenient mechanism by which the various crises of the human relationships could be resolved. Star Trek, the film-makers are saying, is actually a classy soap opera with a futuristic mise en scene:

"What struck me as engaging about the original series," Meyer stated, "is that it wasn't really a science fiction show. It was a show about certain moral and ethical dilemmas that were placed before our Trek characters. Questions concerning life, death, meaning, honor and friendship were brought up in every episode. This movie tries to echo that concept with greater sophistication and depth."

Whether the conclusion reached by Meyer is accurate or not, it shows how open to interpretation Star Trek is and how the show has charted its own destiny no matter how much one may want to recapture the past.

Nicholas Meyer deserves credit, nevertheless, for making *Star Trek II: The Wrath of Khan* enjoyable to watch, thereby not misplacing the faith of the majority of fans. While he professed to have no special affinity for Star Trek, the film appears to be the result of tender loving care.

His style is oriented to dialogue (if all the visuals were removed, leaving only the soundtrack, the story could still be followed like a *Mercury Theatre* radio play) and not to the flashy camera work like Spielberg or Kubrick; even the photographic angles in the television series are less workmanlike. Yet there are few, if any, boring moments in the picture. The action/adventure ingredients, dormant in the first picture, help make *Star Trek II: The Wrath of Khan* the best Star Trek since the end of its second season on the network airwaves.

Designed and Edited by Hal Schuster

JAMES VAN HISE writes about film, television and comic book history. He has written numerous books on these subjects, including BATMANIA, THE TREK CREW BOOK, STEPHEN KING & CLIVE BARKER: THE ILLUSTRATED GUIDE TO THE MASTERS OF THE MACABRE and HOW TO DRAW ART FOR COMIC BOOKS: LESSONS FROM THE MASTERS. He is the publisher of MIDNIGHT GRAFFITI, in which he has run previously unpublished stories by Stephen King and Harlan Ellison. Van Hise resides in San Diego along with his wife, horses and various other animals.

Library of Congress Cataloging-in-Publication Data
James Van Hise, 1949—
    The Best of Enterprise Incidents

    1.   Star Trek (television)
I. Title

Published by Pioneer Books, Inc., 5715 N. Balsam Rd., Las Vegas, NV, 89130.

First Printing, 1990

The Phantom
The Green Hornet
The Shadow
The Batman

Each issue of Serials Adventures Presents offers 100 or more pages of pure nostalgic fun for $16.95

SERIALS ADVENTURES MAGAZINE

Flash Gordon Part One
Flash Gordon Part Two
Blackhawk

Each issue of Serials Adventures Presents features a chapter by chapter review of a rare serial combined with biographies of the stars and behind-the-scenes information. Plus rare photos. See the videotapes and read the books!

UNCLE

THE U.N.C.L.E. TECHNICAL MANUAL

Every technical device completely detailed and blueprinted, including weapons, communications, weaponry, organization, facitilites... 80 pages. 2 volumes...$9.95 each

PRISONER

NUMBER SIX: THE COMPLEAT PRISONER

The most unique and intelligent television series ever aired! Patrick McGoohan's tour-de-force of spies and mental mazes finally explained episode by episode, including an interview with the McGoohan and the complete layout of the real village!...160 pages...$14.95

GREEN HORNET TELEVISION

THE GREEN HORNET

Daring action adventure with the Green Hornet and Kato. This show appeared before Bruce Lee had achieved popularity but delivered fun, superheroic action. Episode guide and character profiles combine to tell the whole story...120 pages...$14.95

WILD, WILD WEST

WILD, WILD, WEST

Is it a Western or a Spy show? We couldn't decide so we're listing it twice. Fantastic adventure, convoluted plots, incredible devices...all set in the wild, wild west! Details of fantastic devices, character profiles and an episode-by-episode guide...120 pages...$17.95

THE COUCH POTATO BOOK CATALOG   5715 N BALSAM, LAS VEGAS, NV   89130

TREK YEAR 1
The earliest voyages and the creation of the series. An in-depth episode guide, a look at the pilots, interviews, character profiles and more...
160 pages...$10.95

TREK YEAR 2
TREK YEAR 3
$12.95 each

THE ANIMATED TREK
Complete inone volume $14.95

THE MOVIES
The chronicle of all the movies...
116 pages...$12.95

STAR TREK

THE LOST YEARS
For the first time anywhere, the exclusive story of the Star Trek series that almost was including a look at every proposed adventure and an interview with the man that would have replaced Spock. Based on interviews and exclusive research...
160 pages...$14.95

NEXT GENERATION
Complete background of the new series. Complete first season including character profiles and actor biographies...160 pages
...$19.95

THE TREK ENCYCLOPEDIA
The reference work to Star Trek including complete information on every character, alien race and monster that ever appeared as well as full information on every single person that ever worked on the series from the stars to the stunt doubles from extras to producers, directors, make-up men and cameramen...**over 360 pages. UPDATED EDITION. Now includes planets, ships and devices**...$19.95

INTERVIEWS ABOARD THE ENTERPRISE
Interviews with the cast and crew of Star Trek and the Next Generation. From Eddie Murphy to Leonard Nimoy and from Jonathan Frakes to Marina Sirtis. Over 100 pages of your favorites.
$18.95

THE ULTIMATE TREK
The most spectacular book we have ever offered. This volume completely covers every year of Star Trek, every animated episode and every single movie. Plus biographies, interviews, profiles, and more. Over 560 pages! Hardcover only. Only a few of these left. $75.00

TREK HANDBOOK and TREK UNIVERSE
The Handbook offers a complete guide to conventions, clubs, fanzines.
The Universe presents a complete guide to every book, comic, record and everything else.
Both volumes are edited by Enterprise Incidents editor James Van Hise. Join a universe of Trek fun!
Handbook...$12.95   Universe...$17.95

THE CREW BOOK
The crew of the Enterprise including coverage of Kirk, Spock, McCoy, Scotty, Uhura,Chekov, Sulu and all the others...plus starship staffing practices...250 pages...$17.95

THE MAKING OF THE NEXT GENERATION: SCRIPT TO SCREEN
THIS BOOK WILL NOT BE PRINTED UNTIL APRIL OR MAY. Analysis of every episode in each stage, from initial draft to final filmed script. Includes interviews with the writers and directors. 240 pages...$14.95

THE COUCH POTATO BOOK CATALOG 5715 N BALSAM, LAS VEGAS, NV   89130

Boring, but Necessary Ordering Information!

Payment: All orders must be prepaid by check or money order. Do not send cash. All payments must be made in US funds only.

Shipping: We offer several methods of shipment for our product.

Postage is as follows:

For books priced under $10.00— for the first book add $2.50. For each additional book under $10.00 add $1.00. (This is per individual book priced under $10.00, not the order total.)

For books priced over $10.00— for the first book add $3.25. For each additional book over $10.00 add $2.00. (This is per individual book priced over $10.00, not the order total.)

These orders are filled as quickly as possible. Sometimes a book can be delayed if we are temporarily out of stock. You should note on your order whether you prefer us to ship the book as soon as available or send you a merchandise credit good for other TV goodies or send you your money back immediately. Shipments normally take 2 or 3 weeks, but allow up to 12 weeks for delivery.

Special UPS 2 Day Blue Label RUSH SERVICE: Special service is available for desperate Couch Potatos. These books are shipped within 24 hours of when we receive your order and should take 2 days to get from us to you.

For the first **RUSH SERVICE** book under $10.00 add $4.00. For each additional 1 book under $10.00 and $1.25. (This is per individual book priced under $10.00, not the order total.)

For the first **RUSH SERVICE** book over $10.00 add $6.00. For each additional book over $10.00 add $3.50 per book. (This is per individual book priced over $10.00, not the order total.)

Canadian and Foreign shipping rates are the same except that Blue Label RUSH SERVICE is not available. All Canadian and Foreign orders are shipped as books or printed matter.

DISCOUNTS! DISCOUNTS! Because your orders are what keep us in business we offer a discount to people that buy a lot of our books as our way of saying thanks. On orders over $25.00 we give a 5% discount. On orders over $50.00 we give a 10% discount. On orders over $100.00 we give a 15% discount. On orders over $150.00 we give a 20% discount. Please list alternates when possible. Please state if you wish a refund or for us to backorder an item if it is not in stock.

100% satisfaction guaranteed. We value your support. You will receive a full refund as long as the copy of the book you are not happy with is received back by us in reasonable condition. No questions asked, except we would like to know how we failed you. Refunds and credits are given as soon as we receive back the item you do not want.

Please have mercy on Phyllis and carefully fill out this form in the neatest way you can. Remember, she has to read a lot of them every day and she wants to get it right and keep you happy! You may use a duplicate of this order blank as long as it is clear. **Please don't forget to include payment! And remember, we** *love* **repeat friends...**

▪▪▪▪▪▪▪▪▪▪▪▪▪▪▪▪▪▪▪▪▪ORDER FORM▪▪▪▪▪▪▪▪▪▪▪▪▪▪▪▪▪▪▪▪▪▪▪▪▪▪▪

_____The Phantom $16.95
_____The Green Hornet $16.95
_____The Shadow $16.95
_____Flash Gordon Part One $16.95 _____Part Two $16.95
_____Blackhawk $16.95
_____Batman $16.95
_____The UNCLE Technical Manual One $9.95 _____Two $9.95
_____The Green Hornet Television Book $14.95
_____Number Six The Prisoner Book $14.95
_____The Wild Wild West $17.95
_____Trek Year One $10.95
_____Trek Year Two $12.95
_____Trek Year Three $12.95
_____The Animated Trek $14.95
_____The Movies $12.95
_____Next Generation $19.95
_____The Lost Years $14.95
_____The Trek Encyclopedia $19.95
_____Interviews Aboard The Enterprise $18.95
_____The Ultimate Trek $75.00
_____Trek Handbook $12.95 _____Trek Universe $17.95
_____The Crew Book $17.95
_____The Making of the Next Generation $14.95
_____The Freddy Krueger Story $14.95
_____The Aliens Story $14.95
_____Robocop $16.95
_____Monsterland's Horror in the '80s $17.95
_____The Compleat Lost in Space $17.95
_____Lost in Space Tribute Book $9.95
_____Lost in Space Tech Manual $9.95
_____Supermarionation $17.95
_____The Unofficial Beauty and the Beast $14.95
_____Dark Shadows Tribute Book $14.95
_____Dark Shadows Interview Book $18.95
_____Doctor Who Baker Years $19.95
_____The Doctor Who Encyclopedia:The 4th Doctor $19.95
_____Illustrated Stephen King $12.95
_____Gunsmoke Years $14.95

NAME:_____

STREET:_____

CITY:_____

STATE:_____

ZIP:_____

TOTAL:_____ SHIPPING_____

SEND TO: COUCH POTATO,INC.
5715 N BALSAM, LAS VEGAS, NV 89130